MURDER WITH LOVE

MURDER WITH LOVE

VECHEL HOWARD

CUTTING EDGE

ISBN-13: 978-1-962896-91-7

Published by
Cutting Edge Books
PO Box 8212
Calabasas, CA 91372
www.cuttingedgebooks.com

For Johnny Roscoe

Herein you'll see
He is not he
And she's not she;
Yet should it fit,
Could be you're it.

CHAPTER ONE

H E ROLLED SOUTH along The Strip in the rented car, a new puce-colored convertible. It was hot in Las Vegas and the pools of the big hotels and motels were crowded with people looking very much like a variety of colorful desert flora. Few swam, he noticed. Mostly they reclined about the perimeters of the sterilized waters, their dark-goggled faces, though all too often quite unflowerlike, all turned like flowers toward the zenith where the sun hung.

At Flamingo Road he made a left turn, crossed Paradise and went on. He watched the signs until he came to Lariat Lane, which the man at the telephone company had said would lead him to Heavenly Knoll. And now, ahead, he could see the knoll, rising like a plump, sand breast from the sage-grown plain, where builders had recently left a geometrical litter of upper-class housing. Atop the knoll there sat, like a pink, sparkling nipple, the ultimate outline of a house.

That, it turned out, was the house he was looking for. Number 10 Heavenly Terrace, occupied by a Mrs. Joy Taliaferro.

A strapping young maid appeared in answer to the subdued notes of the door chimes. The young lady could have stepped out of the chorus line of one of the supper rooms along The Strip, he thought. For that matter maybe she had. She was a vital, buxom creature, all tan, gleaming teeth, sun-bleached, buckskin-colored hair, and a lavish, jutting bosom. There was a far from servile glint in her big, cerulean eyes as she looked him over while he stood there in his sport shirt on the artful flags.

"Hello, honey," she said. "I mean excuse me!" She laughed. "Good afternoon, sir."

He maintained an unsurprisable, professional calm. "I would like to speak to Mrs. Taliaferro, if you please, ma'am," he said.

She moved aside, gliding, jiggling, beckoning him gaily in. "Hear that *ma'am*," she declared under her breath as he stepped past her into the pink-and-white-tiled foyer.

Beyond the foyer was a large, cool-looking room. There a great white rug lay like a light fall of snow upon the tiles, and pastel sleds of couches and low-lying teakwood tables completed the picture. Somewhere within the pink walls of that knoll-top demesne he could hear ladies' voices and there was a sudden splash as someone dived into a pool.

"I guess you better wait in here." The young lady in the fuchsia uniform with the white apron gestured toward the big room, then she preceded him there on high heels, everything vibrating as she walked. "I'm new at the job," she explained. "Guess you can see that. I came for the cure. You know—a divorcee. Figured to get me a job as waitress but I guess plenty others come here with the same idea. *Maid*, the ad said. So I'm giving it a big whirl." She gazed at him. "It's *Mrs.* Taliaferro you want?"

"Yes, ma'am." He handed her one of his business cards, met those great, life-hungering eyes again as she took it. Then he watched her turn, the brief fuchsia skirt swirling up about her full, tanned thighs, and go clicking and bouncing off toward a pair of tall white doors.

When she opened the doors the hot light silhouetted her hips and legs for an instant through the cotton, blocked off for precious moments the scene framed by the opened doors. He had a glimpse, no more, of one end of a pool, the burning sky, and a pink wall. In the middle of this scene were two nude young ladies of surpassing come-liness, each with a striped towel draped about her neck, each rubbing gently upward at her close-cropped curls. For an instant the door let in their voices, their laughter; then the doors closed and he stood bemused, wondering if he had really seen them.

There was a flicker of movement in a doorway at the end of the room and he turned his head to see a man standing there looking in at him, a squat, heavy-set man. He was dressed in a khaki bush jacket and Bermuda shorts, and had on a beret. He was a dark-complexioned fellow with thick, hairy legs, standing there gazing in at him with a complete lack of expression on his face.

Then, as he and the man regarded each other, there was the sound of the tall white doors opening and he turned his head that way again, hoping to get another look at that charming pair of unclad maidens. But they had vanished. He could see only the sky, the pool, the wall. Then two silhouettes advanced toward him, feminine shapes that took on color and substance as the doors closed behind them. In the lead was a lovely lady in well-filled white velveteen breeches. Following her came the maid.

"That will be all, Letty," said the lady, and the Venus in fuchsia did a smart left face and strutted off across the snowy rug.

This lady's breasts were covered by a double bandoleer, the effect achieved with an Italian print scarf. Her hair was the color of lacquered smoke and it was impossible at first to tell how old she was. She was barefoot and her feet were lovely, slender twin sculptures, each carmine-tipped toe a thing of delicate beauty.

Despite her informality, the entire effect of this little lady was one of immense dignity. Dignity hovered like a bird about her patrician head; yet there was something else. He sensed it. It was like the chill whisper of the air conditioner somewhere behind him, he decided. It was something very cold.

She paused before him, gazed up at him with intense gray-green eyes. She smiled and tapped her white teeth delicately with his card. She didn't look over twenty-eight, he thought, and yet he knew somehow that she was much older. But he was at a loss to know how he knew.

"You're Mrs. Joy Taliaferro?" he asked her.

She nodded. "You're a detective, I gather." She looked at the card, read it: "Gerard Secret Service. Worldwide Detective Agency. John Church, Manager, San Francisco Office."

"Yes, ma'am," he said.

"You're Mr. Church?"

"I am," he said.

The light in the room was easy on the lady. Outside, in the desert brilliance, you might see the hairline scars where her face had been lifted, he thought. And still he felt he could be wrong. The breasts beneath the thin stuff of the scarf were firm and high, the beige skin above the waistband of the velveteen breeches was silky and smooth-looking. Whatever her age, she packed a charge.

"Won't you sit down?" she said, and led him across the snow to one of the pastel sleds. They sank back in the cushions and he lit the cigarette she took from a silver box on the teakwood table. And now, beyond the lighter flame and her bent head, he could see the eastern part of the town lying below them. For an instant he stared out through the windows at that blue distance of thorn and yucca where the monstrous mushroom clouds bloomed. It was the lady's hands that betrayed her, he decided, glancing back at her. Her hands were no longer young.

"What can I do for you?" she asked.

"I'm looking for Mira Whitney," he told her. He was watching her eyes. "You're acquainted with the lady, I believe."

She shook her head slowly. "Never heard of her," she said.

He reached in his hip pocket and took out a small note-book and, as he did, the man who had been standing in the doorway vanished. He turned pages until he came to the one with the telephone number on it. He read Mrs. Taliaferro the number, then he said, "Isn't that the number of your telephone?"

"Yes," she said.

"Mira Whitney telephoned you from the Sands Hotel about ten days ago," he said.

She shook her head again. "There must be some mistake, Mr. Church."

"If it was a mistake," he told her, "she made it several times. There's a record of three calls."

"Perhaps she was trying to reach the people who own the house," Mrs. Taliaferro said. "I only rent, you see."

He gazed at her. "There's no reason for you to be afraid to talk to me," he said. "I only want to locate this Whitney girl."

He watched the lady carefully extinguish the cigarette he had just lit for her. Then she leaned back and closed her eyes and presently two tears appeared beneath her lashes. "What's the poor soul done now?" she whispered.

"Well," he said, "in the first place, she seems to have vanished. My client is a San Francisco businessman. He comes from an old family there. A couple of weeks ago he drove down here to see his wife. She was establishing residence for a divorce and he wanted to get back a ring she had. It's an emerald and diamond ring and it's worth a good deal of money. The point is, though, the ring be-longs in a family trust and the wife wasn't supposed to keep it. She knew that when my client gave it to her as an engagement ring. Anyhow—to be as brief as possible—my Mr. X got the ring back, then he turned around and gave it to this Whitney lady." He gazed at her, wondering why the tears.

Mrs. Taliaferro moved her lovely head slowly from side to side. "Oh, but no," she said.

"But yes," he told her. "Mr. X also bought her a Jag while he was here."

"Men are simply helpless with her," murmured Mrs. Taliaferro.

"It looks that way," he agreed. "They met there by the pool at The Sands. He knew her just four days and they were going to get married as soon as she finished putting in time for her divorce. He went back to San Francisco to get his affairs in order so that he could take off on a nice long honeymoon. Meanwhile, she skipped. He telephoned her at The Sands. She'd checked out. No forwarding address. So he waited a few days, biting his nails, thinking maybe she'd get in touch. When she didn't he came and asked me to find her."

As he concluded this little resume Mrs. Taliaferro rose, and once more he admired the girlish waist, the plump perfection of the velveteen-sheathed *derrière*. He watched as she crossed to a chest against the wall with languid grace, opened a drawer and removed a tissue.

While she dabbed carefully at her eyes with the tissue he said, "Do you know where she is, ma'am?"

"No, I don't," she said. "And I don't think it will do any good to look for her, Mr. Church."

"Why won't it?"

"Because I'm sure you won't find her," she said. She returned to the couch, sank down once more and stretched her arms above her head, her gray-green glance resting upon him.

"Why do you say that?"

"I say it," she said, "because I know she has vanished before and people have looked in vain for her. She did it in Cannes, in Acapulco that I know of. She's ill, Mr. Church. For long periods she will go off to a sanatorium or to some remote hideaway to rest, build up her health. Then for a time she lives with complete intensity. And once more, abruptly she will vanish, just as she has now."

"Does the lady, just before she vanishes, make a practice of accepting expensive gifts from men who think she's going to marry them?"

"I fear so," said Mrs. Taliaferro sadly. "Poor lost creature. I suppose that's how she finances herself."

"You know her pretty well, it would seem," he said.

"She frequents the spas, the resorts," said Mrs. Taliaferro. "Just as I do. For me it must always be summer, and I like it where people are gay. And then, too, I have a passion for roulette. That's why I'm here again in this grotesque and fascinating place for a month or so. But no—I wouldn't say I know her well. One will see her, riding in an open car with a handsome gentleman on the road to Saint-Tropez, her beautiful black hair blowing in the wind. She will enter the casino at Monte Carlo and all heads will turn to watch her. Or she may appear on the afternoon beach at Acapulco. One is acquainted with her, speaks to her; one hears the whispers about her, her illness, her doom, her desperate grasping at life and the way she uses men. Yet I don't think anyone really knows her. She remains very much a mystery."

"If she's pulled this shady trick so often," he said, "I'm surprised somebody hasn't caught up with her by now. A character like that," he added, "should take a rap."

Lovely Lady White Breeches gave him a look and shook her exquisite head. "Oh no, Mr. Church," she said. "I don't think anyone wants to *hurt* her, to give her a rap. Does the man you represent want to?"

"No," he admitted. "He only wants to find her, find out what's with her. You know, why she ran out, and if she's all right."

"He acts more in sorrow or anxiety—even anguish—than in anger, then?"

"That's it."

"Well," she said, "so far as I know, that's typical of others she has left romantically high and dry. There was this man in Cannes, one of those rich new industrialists from West Germany. He fell in love with her and they were to be married, everyone understood, as soon as he got rid of his wife. They say he gave her jewels, securities. And then—"

"She pulled her vanishing act."

Mrs. Taliaferro nodded. "Oh, I tell you, that poor man nearly lost his reason afterward. He hired detectives to try and find her. He neglected his business. For a year he haunted the Riviera looking for her, for someone who might have seen her somewhere. He would ask me each time I encountered him, 'Oh, my dear Mrs. Taliaferro, have you seen my Mira, my Cheever girl?' "

"Cheever?" said Johnny.

"That was the name we always knew her by before."

"Miss or Mrs.?" he asked.

"Miss, I think," Mrs. Taliaferro said after a moment's reflection. "I never really spoke to her until I met her here and people simply referred to her as that Cheever girl. In any event, the poor man in Cannes finally received a note from her. She was in Buenos Aires. He told me she wrote that she was, at the moment, well, and her most precious memory was of the days they had spent together. She had left him, she said, only to spare him tragedy. She begged him not to seek her further."

Mrs. Taliaferro laughed. "I bumped into the fellow just as he was leaving his hotel to return to West Germany," she went on. "And he was *happy*, believe it or not. He was content to know that she was well at the moment and remembered him so fondly. He bore her no malice. Never!" Mrs. Taliaferro loosed another peal of laughter. "Can you imagine that!"

"Why did she phone you?" he asked.

"I was playing roulette at The Sands one night," said Mrs. Taliaferro, "and I looked up and saw her standing across the table. She smiled at me and later we chatted. I asked her to come up for a swim and lunch next day. The next morning she phoned and said she couldn't come that day but would the day after be all right. I said it would. Then the next day she again phoned and begged off. Something had come up, she said. Her plans were very uncertain. And, naturally, I assumed she had begun an affair with another man."

He nodded. "That's where my client came in, I guess."

"The last time she phoned it was to say she was going away and to ask me if I would care to buy her Jaguar. I declined. I might have bought it for my girls, but I knew how they would fight over who would drive."

"You have girls old enough to drive a car, ma'am?"

She nodded. "Twin girls."

"I just wouldn't believe that."

"You flatter me, sir," she said.

He rose then, remembering the two at the poolside, wishing those tall white doors hadn't closed behind the bouncy maid quite so quickly. "Well, ma'am," he declared, "I want to thank you for what you've been able to tell me. Now I'll be going."

At the front door, to which Mrs. Taliaferro escorted him, he turned and said to her, looking directly into those big gray-green eyes, "You wouldn't have any idea at all where I might find the lady right now?"

"No," Mrs. Taliaferro said. "I think you are wasting your time, Mr. Church. From what I know of her I'm quite sure you won't find her. Certainly not in Las Vegas."

CHAPTER TWO

COMING DOWN the breast of sand from that sexy pink house in Heavenly Acres he saw a station wagon sweep out from somewhere behind the house. When he turned toward The Strip he saw the station wagon in his rear-view mirror, turning too.

The lady's story, he thought, even though dealing with such an exotic, fabulous subject, had been essentially plausible and in accord with what information he had. All but Mrs. Taliaferro's tears was understandable. She just wasn't that emotional.

Why, he wondered, the tears?

And, if Mira Whitney had really come there for a divorce, what had scared her away? Certainly not his client.

He drove to the county courthouse, parked and went in. When he looked through the record of divorce actions pending, under the W's, he found the name of Mira Cheever Whitney, who was seeking a divorce from Alan K. Whitney. Mrs. Whitney's address was given as in care of her attorneys, Temple, Beecroft and Spigner, on Fremont Street; Mr. Whitney's address was in Chicago. Mrs. Whitney had about ten day's time left to serve on her six-week residence period.

Along Fremont Street the neon signs were glowing at midday, the slot machines were jangling, silver dollars clinking on green felt-covered tables. In the bars, rows of sport-shirted men perched like bright-hued vultures on their stools, staring out at the sun-smitten street. Above all the other sounds, there was always the constant, cadenced calling of numbers from the bingo games.

In a small office building, a minor, gray-stone austerity amid the incandescence, Temple, Beecroft and Spigner had their office. It was an air-conditioned temple of the law on the second floor front, where a deeply-tanned secretary in a sheath cotton print and a ponytail hair-do sat filing her nails, her feet propped up on her desk, gazing down upon the crowded and noisy street with profound boredom showing in her slanty brown eyes.

"Good afternoon, ma'am," said Johnny. He stood there with the door sighing shut behind him while the girl in the spectator pumps unhurriedly lowered her legs to the floor. "I'd like to see the lawyer who is handling Mrs. Whitney's case," he told the lady.

"Whitney," she repeated. She knew the name. It showed in her eyes as she continued to gaze at him. "One moment please," she finally said. She rose then, flowed up out of her chair, smoothed the print stuff over her thighs and moved across the carpeting to a door.

"Your name?" she asked, turning.

"Church."

When the lady vanished through the door he sat down and lit a cigarette. He knew from previous experience it was a tough town to do business in. He guessed it always had been. In the beginning there had been the rattlesnakes to distract a man from his duty. Now there were the ladies.

In a moment the girl in the print sheath reappeared and held open the door for him. She gave him a slow, damp-looking smile. "Mr. Beecroft will see you," she said.

"Thank you." He got up and just managed to get past her without stabbling himself on her breasts.

"First office on your left, honey," she murmured in the friendly way they had there in Las Vegas after they had known you for a few minutes.

In that town everything was dear, darling, honey and even precious. The only time you had to watch it or think anything about it was if parties of the same gender should start to talk to you that way.

The office on the left was big, the desk was big, and so was the man behind the desk. He got up as Johnny entered, stuck out a hand, and said with a sunny, Western smile, "Ah'm Gene Beecroft. Howdy, Mr. Church." And the wide-open spaces were reflected in this genial fellow's face, in his garb, his tall, lank figure. But when you gazed into the small, slate-colored eyes you knew that there were still snakes around.

"Sit down," Mr. Beecroft went on, tugging at his black string tie and giving a hacking cough. "What can ah do you for?"

That last sentence was said starting on a high note, then letting the following words glide soapily downscale. Johnny had the feeling as they seated themselves that the lawyer had just stroked him gently, looking for concealed weapons, maybe, or just setting him up for a sneaky left hook later on.

He came to the point without delay. "I'm a private investigator," he said. "My client, a man in San Francisco, wants me to locate a Mrs. Whitney, first name Mira, formerly Mira Cheever. I understand you are representing her in a divorce action here."

"That's right," Beecroft agreed placidly.

"Do you know where she is?"

"Naturally ah do," Beecroft said.

"Can you give me her address?"

"Ah could maybe, Mr. Church, but ah sure ain't going to do so." Beecroft swung a pair of highly polished cowboy boots up on his desk and rubbed at his bristly red hair. "No, sir," he declared. "You come knocking at the wrong door."

"Maybe I better explain," Johnny told him. "My client planned to marry the lady. He bought her a Jag. He gave her a valuable ring. She was staying at The Sands and she disappeared."

"Ah just don't believe a word of that," Beecroft told him. "Must have been some other lady that was involved, my friend. Ah *know* my client and, believe me, any such allegations concerning her are simply unthinkable." He swung his boots off the desk and leaned forward. His face had gotten red. "Ah *resent* those allegations," he said. "Ah just don't believe one damn thing you tell me, friend. Ah know who's paying you."

"Who?" Johnny asked.

Beecroft stood up. "Whitney's paying you. That jealous, no-good husband of hers is forking up your fee." He leaned forward and the slate-colored eyes appeared suddenly lidless. "Now just let me tell you something," he went on. "First, you git your big carcass out of that chair of mine; then you git back to where you come from and you tell that *client* of yours 'No dice.' If you go nosing around trying to bother a certain little lady ah'll have 'em pick you up on a vagrancy charge. You want to spend some time in our jail?"

"No," Johhny said.

"Then, friend," Beecroft whispered, "take my advice. *Git!*"

When he came back through the door into the outer office the girl in the sheath dress was just gliding hastily away from the door toward her desk.

Johnny stopped and looked at her and she raised her brows quizzically. She had eavesdropped; she knew what he wanted to know.

"Ma'am—"he began, then he stopped. The door he had just come through had opened again and Beecroft was standing there.

"I thought I advised you to git," said Beecroft softly.

"I am," Johnny told him. "I was just about to ask this lady the shortest way out of town." He turned abruptly and left the office.

He went down the stairs and walked along Fremont Street for a couple of blocks, then he crossed the street and started back. Pausing to look in the window of a haberdashery store, he could see the opposite side of the street reflected in the glass. He could see a figure in a bush jacket and Bermuda shorts. It was the man with the beret from the pink house in Heavenly Acres. He had also paused to look in a window.

John Church continued along the street and he did not stop again until he came to the bar directly across from the building where Beecroft's office was. Before entering the bar he looked up at the second-floor window where the ponytail sat filing her nails. After a moment she looked at him across the bright street. The lady favored him with that slow, damp-looking smile of hers and he tried to pack a lot of meaning in the look he gave her before he turned and went into the bar.

He spent the remainder of the afternoon pleasantly enough. He took his time in losing twenty-four dollars playing blackjack in the gambling room adjacent to the bar. Then he sat at the bar drinking a beer, gazing out the window at the garish parade of people, glancing up at the lawyer's lady now and then.

Meanwhile, he thought about the one he was looking for, and realized that everything he had heard about that lady fascinated him. She had intrigued him right from the start, ever since his client, a middle-aged businessman named Hamilton Sprague, had told him about her over a Green Goddess salad at the Palace Hotel in San Francisco at lunch the day before.

"It isn't necessarily that I even want to get the ring back from her," Sprague had told him. "I don't care if she keeps the ring. I can have a duplicate made. I don't care about the car, either. I just want to find her, that's all. I want to make sure she's all right. And I'd like to know *why*—why did she run out on me? Something must have happened. I want to know. I've *got* to know."

Johnny had avoided looking at Mr. Sprague because the older man had become so worked up telling about it that there were tears glistening behind his glasses. Sprague was pushing fifty, and his story was a fairly familiar one to Johnny Church. Old guy, young girl. Girl takes guy. He had tried to bring the case down from the high emotional level where the aesthetic-looking Sprague had put it to a more matter-of-fact one. First, he had asked where the lady came from. Sprague had said he thought she was from New York. One of her great attractions for him, he said, had been her refusal to discuss backgrounds or the past. She had wished to live completely in an intense and splendid present, yet of course it had been evident to him that she was a highly cultivated, intelligent girl who had traveled widely and must have come from a very fine family.

"Can you describe her?" Johnny had asked him.

"Describe her?" Sprague echoed. He had grown quite dreamy looking as he said it.

"Could you tell me the color of her hair, for instance?"

"Black—" Sprague had declared in a rapt and sorrowing voice. "Black as the proverbial raven's wing. The glossiest, most beautiful hair in the world."

"Eyes?"

"Dark—no, bluish, I guess. But you think of them as dark, deeply dark with sheer feeling. There's so much of life and passion in them, such awareness of the transient nature of life."

"She seems to have been transient all right."

Mr. Sprague had paid no attention to the remark. "She reminded me of a bird I once held in my hand," he had continued. "When I was a boy I found this beautiful little bird with a broken wing and I'll never forget the feeling I got when I picked it up—the feeling of tremendous, vibrant life trapped in that frail body."

"She was frail?"

"Well, no. Lovely figure. Oh, gorgeous! But somehow she just gave me that impression. The bird got away from me and flew into some brush where I couldn't find it." Mr. Sprague had paused, blinking back tears again. "I suppose it died there. And now I've got that terrible, tragic feeling about her. I shouldn't have left her. I felt somehow she didn't have long to live. Now that I've had time to think about it I realize I could sense that in everything she said and did, despite her wonderful gaiety."

"What seemed to be wrong with her?"

"I don't know exactly." Mr. Sprague had taken out a handkerchief and blown his nose. He had then ordered another vodka on the rocks.

It had subsequently been established that the lady in question was about twenty-five years old, about five-feet-five inches tall and weighed perhaps one-hundred-twenty pounds. And before the conclusion of the luncheon Johnny had said to Mr. Sprague, "Excuse me, but if I'm to do this investigation for you I should possess what few facts are available. Did you have relations with her?"

"Eh?" Mr. Sprague had asked him absently.

"Did you lay the lady?"

"No," Mr. Sprague had said, flushing, more with chagrin and regret, it had appeared, than with embarrassment.

CHAPTER THREE

A BOUT A QUARTER TO FIVE Beecroft, wearing a white Stetson hat, came out of the office building across the street with another man. The two got into a car and drove off; then, promptly at five o'clock, the ponytail appeared once more at her window. While she sat holding a mirror and repairing her lipstick he walked over and stood at the bar door and they exchanged another look. When the lady vanished, he went to a rear booth and sat down facing the street and presently she entered, came and seated herself opposite him.

Glancing beyond her now at the doorway, he saw a figure pause in the bright street, hesitate and move on. It was the one in the bush jacket and the beret again.

A waitress came. "What'll you dears have?" she asked.

"A screwdriver, doll," said the lady.

"For me a beer." He gazed into the slanty brown eyes, watched the tip of a pink tongue emerge and slide slowly along over the full red upper lip. "Thanks for coming," he said. He knew what she was doing. She was sizing him up, estimating how much he would be good for.

She smiled finally. "What can I do for you?" she asked.

"I want that Whitney girl's address," he said.

She continued to smile. "What makes you think you'll get it from me?"

"Twenty bucks," he suggested.

She shook her head. "It could be worth my job, honey."

He shrugged. "There are other ways to find out," he said. Their drinks came then and he picked up his beer, his eyes meeting hers once more as they drank.

She downed her screwdriver in one long, unladylike gulp and stood up. "Thanks for the drink," she told him.

He sighed. "Sit down," he said, and after a moment she did. He gazed at her. "You saw Mira Whitney?"

"I saw her," she said.

"What's she got? The way I hear it the boys take one look at her and check their wits."

She shook her head thoughtfully. "She's beautiful," she said. "She's got a figure. But it isn't just her looks. Something about her makes you watch her. You feel maybe something important's going to happen when she comes into a room. Do you get what I mean, honey? It's like some big actress. You ever seen an old Garbo picture?"

He nodded. *"Camille* I saw."

"Yeah," she said. "Well, that Garbo had what this Whitney dame's got. Even Gene Beecroft fell for it—whatever it is. He's been sending her flowers, trying to date her, phoning her all the time."

"When did he talk to her last?"

"I wouldn't know that," she said.

He figured she was lying. "You would know her address though?"

"I would," she said, "but I'm telling you I could get fired for giving it to you. Look, suppose you make some trouble for this Whitney dame and she tells Beecroft. Then Beecroft's going to want to know how you located her."

"He'll never find out from me," he said. "And anyhow, I'm not going to make any trouble for the lady."

"Beecroft's real mean," she told him. "Don't fool with him. If he said for you to git, honey, you better. He swings a lot of weight in this town."

She went on, building her price up and he let her talk and it turned out she wanted a hundred for Mira Whitney's address. She knew what it was worth to him. She also knew it wasn't his money he was spending, but some rich client's and in the end he paid her price. Then, with the bills in her purse, she told him something else.

"Beecroft hasn't been able to get in touch with her for two days," she said. "Her landlady hasn't seen her." She got up then, giving him that slow, damp smile again. "The lady," she concluded, "appears to have vanished."

He watched her walk out, saw the hourglass figure silhouetted against the late-afternoon light as she stepped into the street. Then, playing it safe, he went back through the kitchen of the place and came out into an alleyway. From there he entered the kitchen of another bar-restaurant and passed on through, emerging on a side street.

The sun had fallen behind that withered Western range of sheep-dung-colored mountains as he drove out The Strip to his motel. By the time he had showered and put on a light suit, with the Magnum .357 strapped on beneath his jacket, dusk had fallen and a dry little wind had sprung up.

The address was across town in North Las Vegas. Now The Strip and the central streets of the town were a neon glow in the dusk. He knew the night people would be dressing, drinking their cocktails, preparing to dine. The croupiers and dealers would be stacking chips, riffling cards, the bartenders squeezing out a supply of lemon juice, the shapely ladies in the floorshows sitting around their dressing rooms deshabille before getting into their costumes. It was night. He had Mira Whitney's address and he could feel his pulses quickening. For him, in his work, the ladies had lost most of their mystery, their glamor; he had seen too many of them in circumstances cruel and clear. Yet with this Whitney girl it was different. He sensed her difference, was aware of his own unprofessional eagerness to track her down, to encounter her in the flesh.

The apartment house in which the lady lived, or had lived, was on Panamint Drive apartment 10B and, though the buildings along that street were new, they did not possess the stark, overnight newness of the Heavenly Acres developement. Here at least, Bermuda grass, trees and shrubs had had a chance to grow.

He parked beneath a pepper tree and turned out the car lights. For a while he studied the apartment house, a frame ranch-style structure build like an airplane, with a central unit and two lateral wings. There were garages beneath the wings and the front doors of the apartments above the garages opened on balconies. There were ten apartments in each wing and the B wing was on his right. 10B was at the end of the balcony. He could just make out the two chrome numerals and the letter glistening in the balcony light. The windows of that apartment were dark.

He was about to open the car door and get out when he noticed the glow of a cigarette inside the sedan parked in the deep shadows along the curb across the street. He waited a moment more, then started the car, switched on his lights and drove around the block. There was a vacant lot at the back of the apartment house and beyond the lot he could see that there were also balconies at the rear of the building and steps leading down to garbage cans and a parking area.

The street light on the corner cast his shadow before him as he got out of the car and stepped across the side-walk into the vacant lot. He had a flashlight in one hand. There was sand in the lot that trickled into his shoes and dried clover burrs caught on his trouser legs. He stopped and listened when he got to the rear steps, then he sat down and emptied the sand from his shoes. And now from the apartments above he could hear a clatter of dishes, a woman's laughter, the blare of a television set. A Western film was in progress and when he relaced his shoes he went on up the steps to the sound of pounding hoofs and gunfire.

There was a window next to the rear door of 10B and through the slats of the blind he could make out the pale, enameled gleam of a stove in the darkness. There was a bell beside the door and he pressed it, waited as the sound died away inside. Next he tried the knob, found the door locked, but that lock was no problem. It took him less than two minutes with a strip of celluloid to spring it, then he was in. He flashed his light around the little kitchen, found it clean, sterile, unused-looking. The living room, furnished in Swedish modern, was the same. There wasn't a book nor a magazine, the wastebasket beneath the empty writing desk was empty, the ashtrays were clean.

In the bedroom, however, it was different. As soon as he stepped through the door he could smell the haunting, exotic scent she used and there was an intense, feminine aura—an effluvium composed of her bath powder, of her lotions, her clothing. For a moment it was as if she were there, as if he were seeing her face in the beam of his flashlight. He was almost on the verge of succumbing to whatever strange magic she possessed.

There was expensive luggage with foreign labels in the closet as well as her clothes. There were evening gowns, suits and dresses and there was also a rack of shoes, size 6A, all of French or Italian make, and the dresser drawers were filled with exquisite articles of intimate apparel. Then, flashing his light at the top of the dresser, he saw the silver-framed photograph, a picture of a young girl. The girl was standing before a low wall on a terrace over-looking the sea and the breeze from the sea was stirring the ends of her black, lustrous hair. She was about fifteen or sixteen and surpassingly beautiful, yet it was not her beauty alone that stabbed his heart. It was the quality of her expression, which was at once pure and wistful, even ethereal, yet still vital and intense. Here in the same lush, lovely package, he thought, were fire and also tenderness, innocence and profound understanding. He gazed with a sense of enchantment at her lips, sensed her passion—for love, for life. Her lips appeared to thirst for kisses, for lovely words to utter.

She was Mira, he knew. He knew it even before he picked up the photograph, took the back off the frame and read the inscription: *Mira on the terrace at Antibes, April '48.*

There was also an ashtray on the dressertop with a half-smoked Egyptian cigarette in it, lipstick on the gold tip. And there was a jewel box. The box was of dark blue leather and bore the initials *M.C.* in gold. He thought he might find the ring his client had given the lady in there, but the box proved to contain only costume jewelry. In the bottom layer of the box, however, there was a piece of photostat paper. It was a copy of a birth certificate for Mira Taliaferro, a female, white, who had been born in France at Saint Tropez, province of Var, some twenty-six years before.

Taliaferro. He stared at the photostat a long moment, then returned it to the box and went out. He recrossed the living room and re-entered the little kitchen. At the back door he snapped off the flashlight and stood a moment with his hand on the doorknob listening, hearing again a sound of gunfire, a frantic pounding of hoofs.

When he opened the door there was a swath of early stars in the sky above the vacant lot. Then there was a rustle of movement to his left and a blow he could neither parry nor avoid was falling on him. Steel came crashing down on his head and there were brief flames of pain and light. After that there was only the cool, black night once more, with the stars now slowly pinwheeling and dancing in the infinite sky.

CHAPTER FOUR

A GAIN HE COULD HEAR the hoofs, the gunfire, and there was also the sound of a drum. Now in his mind he could see the familiar celluloid scene, horsemen racing along a dusty Western road, the eternal pursuers and the pursued. Then a confusion came over him—why was he still there in that dark kitchen on Panamint Road? Why was he sitting down, and why did his head ache so?

At that point he remembered the blow and he realized that he was in an air-conditioned room, a room where there was light. He could discern the light through his eyelids and after a moment he lifted his eyelids a little and took a look.

It was a beautiful room, furnished in a vaguely Oriental style. Anyhow, the long coffee table in front of the huge white couch appeared to be a Chinese piece and there was a white screen with a pagoda scene on it. A young blonde lady clad in a man's pink shirt and, so far as he could see, nothing more, was slumped on the couch beating on a bongo drum with a pair of swizzle sticks. She had a bored, petulant look and an instant after he opened his eyes she stopped her drumming and declared, "For the love of heaven, will you God-damn delinquents turn that thing off?"

No one answered her. Then, moving his head a little, he saw the two young men. They were seated at a table eating sandwiches and drinking beer while they watched the television screen.

"If you guys wanta be cowboys why the hell don't you go *be* cowboys!" the lady in the pink shirt yelled. She picked up the drink that was on the coffee table in front of her and tilted it to her lips.

The two at the table had removed their jackets and hung them over the backs of their chairs. They had on sport shirts and they wore shoulder holsters packing small automatics. One was blond, the other dark and they both wore their hair long, in a swept-wing style, with forelocks. Their faces were smooth and completely devoid of expression. They were sitting so that they could watch both the television set and him.

His hands were not tied. They were lying in his lap and he could see his notebook, his wallet and his gun lying on the table where the two sat. After a moment he shut his eyes again, waiting, and presently he heard a door open.

Then, lifting one eyelid imperceptibly, he saw someone familiar, an aging young man with a tough, likable face and a boyish-looking shock of bronze hair. He was standing in the doorway in a white dinner jacket and he was looking at John Church.

"Mitch—" the two at the table greeted the newcomer. They rose, as if in the presence of royalty, and one of them turned off the television set.

Beyond Mitch he could glimpse shrubbery. He could smell the fragrant desert night coming through the opened door and now he knew they must be in a cottage on the grounds of the Nevada Grande, the newest and plushest of the hotels along The Strip. At the Nevada Grande, Mitch Barry, a pop singer turned moving-picture actor, was heading the floor show. Driving along The Strip that morning on his way to Heavenly Acres he had seen the life-size photograph of Barry mounted in a display case at the entrance to the hotel drive. "Featuring The Incomparable Mitch Barry," the display had said.

Now the incomparable Barry shut the door and came into the room. "He still cold?" he asked. "Maybe you guys hit too hard."

"Mitch," the lady in the pink shirt said, "what goes here?" She had gotten up too.

"Girl," Barry said, glancing at her, "take my shirt off and get dressed, will you? Then go to your room a while. I'll call you later. I've got business now."

"Who are these goons?" the lady asked, pointing to the two standing by the table.

"They're not goons," Mitch told her. "They're my friends. Go on, will you." He moved over, grinned at her and slapped her on her rump.

"Who's this big guy?" she asked, pointing at Johnny.

"That's the sixty-four-thousand-dollar question," Mitch said. "Now hurry it up, will you?" He turned his back on her and, as he stepped toward Johnny, Johnny opened his eyes and gazed at him and he stopped. "So—" he said. He stared at Johnny and his eyes were hot.

In the silence they could hear the lady cursing in the bedroom as she dressed. "Let's see that wallet," Barry said. He went over to the table and the dark young man handed the wallet to him.

"He's a private eye," the dark one said. "His license is there."

Barry took the license out of Johnny's wallet and looked at it. He also examined the gun permit and Johnny's driver's license. As he returned these to the wallet the young lady emerged from the bedroom wearing a white, strapless dress and dragging an evening scarf along behind her. Barry took her to the door and stepped outside with her, stood whispering to her while dance music floated through the sage-and-oleander-laden air from the hotel. Meanwhile, the two strolled over from the table and stood in front of Johnny. After a minute Barry, wiping lipstick from his mouth, came back in and joined them.

"Where's that picture?" Barry asked Johnny.

Johnny shook his head slowly. "You got the wrong boy," he said.

The blond one stepped forward then and slapped him, slapped him hard, and as he started to lunge up from the chair, the dark one got into the act, smashing a fist into his face.

"All right," he told himself while the lights danced again in his head, "don't be crazy. Right now they got all the cards." He pulled a handkerchief from the breast pocket of his jacket and held it to his nose. It was bleeding.

When he opened his eyes he saw the blond one handing Barry a sheet of writing paper, the dark one handing him a magazine. Then Barry took a pen from his pocket and shoved it at him with the magazine and the paper. "Print me something," Barry said.

Johnny took the pen, the paper and the magazine with one hand. He laid the magazine with the writing paper on top of it on his knees and, still holding the handkerchief to his nose, he pondered a moment, then wrote in printed capitals: THE QUICK BROWN FOX JUMPS OVER THE LAZY DOG.

"Now print fifty-thousand dollars in numerals," Barry said.

As soon as he finished Barry snatched the paper and went over and laid it on the table. Then he took an envelope from his pocket, unfolded the letter in it and spread it out beside what Johnny had done.

Presently he returned and handed the letter to Johnny. "You write this?" he asked.

Johnny took the letter, read the simple, slightly puzzling message, printed in pencil on a sheet of ruled notepaper. "LIKE TO SEE THE HEADS?" the message asked. "GET $50,000 READY QUICK. DON'T BE CUTE OR YOU'LL SEE THE PIC—WITH HEADS—IN YOU KNOW WHAT MAGAZINE."

Now Barry handed him a photograph, a picture of a couple, male and female, in bed, only partially concealed by a sheet. The heads of the pair had been cut out.

Johnny looked up at Barry. "You?"

"Yeah." Barry's eyes were still hot-looking.

"Who's the lady?"

"As if you didn't know," Barry said.

"When was the picture taken?"

"Monday night," said Barry.

"I just got in town this morning," Johnny told him. "That I can prove."

"You could go away and come back."

"I can prove I didn't do that. I'm here on legitimate business. What makes you think *I'd* go for blackmail? I'm bonded. I'm licensed."

"For fifty G's?" Barry said contemptuously. "You don't make that peeking through keyholes, mister. And you've been tailing her."

Johnny gazed at him a moment, then he said, "You mean the Whitney lady?" And when Barry nodded, he asked him calmly, "Can you tell me how I could have been tailing her when I haven't even found her yet?"

"Who hired you to find her?" Barry asked.

"A man in San Francisco," Johnny said.

"Why?" Barry demanded.

"She was supposed to marry the guy."

Barry stared at him. "Can you prove it?"

He nodded. His nose had stopped bleeding now. "Let me use your phone and hand me my wallet," he said.

Barry's dark friend got his wallet off the table and flung it in his lap. Johnny took out Hamilton Sprague's card with his office and residence telephone numbers written on it, but as he reached for the telephone that stood on the table beside his chair Barry said. "Okay. Never mind."

Johnny glanced up at him. "You don't want me to call?"

Barry shook his head. "I'll buy your story," he said. He gazed gloomily for a moment at his gun-toting friends. "You two take a walk for yourselves," he told them.

The two stared bleakly at Johnny, then they crossed to the table, put on their jackets and went out.

Mitch Barry sat down on the couch and lit a cigarette. He laid the extortion note and the mutilated photograph on the coffee table in front of him and stared at them.

"When did you get that letter?" Johnny asked him.

"This morning," Barry said. "It was mailed here in Las Vegas at five o'clock yesterday afternoon." His eyes narrowed. "What's this about her being supposed to get married again?"

"First," Johnny said, "I should tell you that the lady has kind of a shady history." He shifted his weight in the chair and explored the left side of his head gently with his fingertips. There was a lump there, dried blood in his hair.

"What do you mean by that?" Barry demanded.

"It seems she has the habit of relieving the boys of valuable gifts, promising to marry them, then disappearing. And she's so good at it nobody gets mad at her." He told Barry about his client's experience with Mira Whitney and also a little of what Mrs. Taliaferro had said about her.

"I don't believe it," Mitch Barry said. "I've played around a lot, mister, and I've been married three times. I'm bone dry behind the ears as far as women are concerned, and I just don't believe it."

"What did she take *you* for?"

"Nothing!"

Johnny shook his head. Not yet, you mean, he thought. He gazed at the letter. "Fifty G's," he reflected. "That's a good round sum." He gazed at Barry. "How did you meet her?"

"I met her last Friday out by the pool here at the hotel," Barry said. "We'd just finished a rehearsal for the show I'm in now and

I'm sitting out there with my agent. She's alone. As usual, people are coming up getting my autograph." Barry paused. "You know how it is."

"I can visualize the scene," said Johnny.

"Well," Barry went on, "whenever *she* glances my way it's as if I'm not there or am maybe just an ashtray or something. And naturally this treatment intrigues me—not to mention her looks. So pretty soon I go over to her and introduce myself. I ask her if she would care to join me for a drink." He paused. "You know my reputation, no doubt."

Johnny nodded. "I read the piece on you in that you-know-what magazine."

"The hell of it was, that piece was true," said Barry. "Just one more item about me in that nasty little sheet and I'm dead." He tapped the photograph. "This, with the heads, could kill me. My studio would break my contract."

"So you got the lady in bed," Johnny mused. He remembered that vital, lovely face. He smelled that haunting scent again, and he was aware of another layer added to the veneer of his disillusion.

"I got her in bed, period," Barry said. "Listen—believe it or not—that's all. She was driving me crazy. I'm still that way. I tell you, I've got to find her."

Johnny regarded him thoughtfully. And he suddenly felt better. The lady took all, gave nothing; that was the pattern. He was searching for a lovely sadist, following a will-o'-the wisp trail strewn with duped yet still love-smitten victims. And it occurred to him now that she must really hate men.

"Anyhow," Barry continued, "just about the time something interesting *might* have happened, the door pops open and some-body snaps that flash picture."

"You see him at all?" Johnny asked.

"No," said Barry. "The room was dark. All I saw was the flash. Then the guy was gone before I could get to the front door."

"What time was this?"

"About two o'clock Monday night, or Tuesday morning. After my last show."

"Where were your gun-toting pals at the time?"

Barry shrugged. "I had no use for them. They were in the casino." He ran a hand through his hair, gazing at Johnny. "What do I do now, mister?"

"What happened after the guy snapped the picture?"

Barry told him that by the time he ran from the bedroom and across the living room to the front door the man had vanished into the night. Then he had to go back into the bedroom to get some clothes on. In the bedroom he found Mira Whitney already dressing and looking very scared and shaken. She said she was sure her husband was having her followed and was behind the picture-taking.

Whitney was insanely jealous, she said. He didn't want the divorce and she was sure he was trying to get something on her.

Johnny shook his head. "That doesn't add up to Whitney black-mailing you."

"I never thought it did," Barry said. "I figured he could have hired somebody to watch her, and that party could have got the blackmail idea on his own."

"Could be," Johnny agreed. It was one of three possibilities he saw at the moment. The second possibility was that there were plenty of characters around Hollywood and Las Vegas who were constantly on the watch for somebody like Mitch Barry to make a misstep. These characters were tough, professional and careful. They took pictures and they got paid off. The third possibility was that Mira Whitney had an accomplice and was in on it. And yet he had to admit that it didn't sound like her, or what he had heard about her.

"Well," he said to Barry, "when did she vanish on you?"

"When I got dressed and came back here into the living room," Barry told him, "she was gone. I thought she was waiting for me, but she ran out. I didn't know where she lived—she wouldn't tell me. I didn't even know her phone number."

"How did you find her apartment?"

"My boys asked around among the taxi drivers. She always traveled by taxi. They located the apartment, but she wasn't there. Manager of the place didn't know where she was. He said her stuff was still there. So I had my boys stake out and wait for her. She wouldn't go away for good and leave her stuff." Barry looked at him hopefully. "Would she? And how about the divorce she's supposed to be getting?"

Johnny shook his head. "You know as much as I do," he said. He stood up.

"What do I do?" Barry demanded. He tapped the decapitated photograph. "I'm on the griddle, man."

"Go to the D.A.," Johnny advised him; then he instantly thought better of it. Cops would be on her trail then. She'd be in trouble. And his client didn't want her in trouble.

Barry was shaking his head. "I can't do that. It would get out. And, besides, they'd be after *her.*"

"Well," Johnny said, "you could pay the fifty G's."

"I haven't got it," Barry said. "I'm an alimony slave. And, besides that, even if I got the negative of that picture, how could I ever be sure they hadn't made a lot of prints? They could keep right on bleeding me."

"It's been my experience they usually do," Johnny told him.

"Okay!" Barry said. "You're a detective. *Advise* me."

Johnny crossed to the table and picked up his gun and his notebook. "They'll be phoning you," he said. "When they do stall them. Tell them to call you back a little later, then get in touch with me." He told Barry the name of his motel.

"You're going to keep trying to find her, aren't you?" Barry asked.

"I *am* going to find her," Johnny assured him.

"Then you'll be working for me, too," Barry suggested. "Right?"

"Not so fast," he told him. "We'll have to see about that, Mr. Barry."

He turned abruptly then and went out. The way he figured it was that he already had a client and he had a job to do for him, namely: find her. And the only justification he would have for getting mixed up in Mitch Barry's trouble was that it might lead him to her. But at the moment it seemed very clear to him that the road that would lead him to her was the same one you took to get to that pink house on the knoll and that was the one he intended to take without delay.

His car was still up there in North Las Vegas behind the Panamint Drive apartment house and he took a taxi to get it. As the taxi went past the apartment house he thought for a minute that the lights were on in 10B and he had the driver stop. Then he saw that the lights weren't in her apartment, but the one next to it.

The taxi went on around the block and he paid the driver and got in his car. He had driven about halfway down the block when the lights of another car swung around the corner behind him. He didn't think anything much about it until he turned off North Main onto Fifth and those lights followed him. There was still nothing very suspicious about that, but he was wary and at the corner of Bonanza he made a little test. He turned back toward

Main, and at that point he was pretty sure he had a tail because the car turned west with him.

He did a little artful dodging then on the side streets and eventually came back to Fifth. He was pretty sure he was in the clear by then, although there were so many cars at that hour—a little after nine o'clock—and all streaming toward The Strip, that he could not be entirely certain. In any event, he went on to his motel to change his bloody shirt and phone the little lady in the pink house.

He gave the switchboard operator the number. It was the lovely lady's voice that answered the phone. "This is Mr. Church," he told her. "I have some information that I'm sure will be of interest to you, Mrs. Taliaferro."

"What information?" she asked.

"I can't tell you over the phone."

"I'm just going out," she said. "Really Mr. Church, I told you all I know about that person. I don't want to be involved further."

"This *does* involve you," he said.

She was silent a moment. "Very well," she declared crisply. "Come in the morning, but not before eleven." She hung up.

He thought of phoning her back, of pressing her to make it that night, but he knew it would be wrong. He wasn't the law. She didn't have to let him into that pink house, didn't have to tell him anything. And having her clam up wouldn't help.

He picked up the phone again and ordered a double high-ball from the motel bar and a steak from the grill. Then he undressed and went into the bathroom to take a shower.

He was drying himself and at the same time peering at the split in his scalp in the bathroom mirror when he heard a movement in the other room. It was the waiter already, he thought, and he put on his robe. Then, as he stepped from the bathroom, a fist hit him, rabbit-punched him, and as he sagged a pair of arms caught him and held him up while other arms pumped away at him, slamming fists to his body. And finally they kneed him, the arms let him go and he slumped to the floor, lay there writhing in a gasping, terrible agony.

By the time the waiter came he had recovered enough to drag himself onto the bed. He gulped the drink the waiter brought and sent him for another. Then he realized that he hadn't even really seen the ones that beat him, but as they left the room one had spoken. "Get out of town," one of them had said.

He had tried to keep a rule; never to get mad on a job no matter what. When you lost your temper you lost your head and maybe loused up the job and yourself. But that rule was overboard now. He lay there burning with a helpless fury. He wanted to kill somebody.

CHAPTER FIVE

WHEN HE WOKE a horn was blaring sharply outside along The Strip and the young palm tree outside his window was groaning and rustling its fronds. When he sat up he also groaned. He got out of bed in a black and bitter mood and for half an hour he soaked his bruises in a hot tub. Then he shaved and dressed and went along to the grill for breakfast.

It was almost eleven when he finished eating. He went to a phone booth in the motel lounge, called Mitch Barry and gave him the Taliaferro number. "I'll be there a while," he told him, "and I'll check with you when I leave."

"When do you think they'll call me?" Barry asked.

"When they're ready to," he snapped. "They're out late, that type, you know—busy taking pictures. Look, Barry, where was that two-headed bodyguard of yours about nine o'clock last night?"

"They were here," Barry said.

"You're sure they weren't staked out around the Whitney apartment?"

"They were here," Barry repeated. "They had dinner and watched my nine-thirty show. They check the apartment a couple of times during the day and a couple of times at night, but they don't stake out there. Why—should they?"

"I don't give a damn what they do," Johnny told him. "Just so they keep out of my way." He hung up.

Barry's two young goons would have clubbed him with their guns, he thought. It really didn't figure to be them. The treatment he had gotten, he knew, had been given by true professionals—cops, ex-cops, or maybe even private detectives—the kind that had learned to half kill a man without marking him up.

Once more at the pink house the bouncy maid opened the door in answer to the chimes. Once more she gave him the bright and hungry eye, the Western warmth of greeting, again she led him into that big, cool room to wait while she went jiggling off to fetch her mistress. But today her charms were lost on him.

Mrs. Taliaferro appeared immediately. She was dressed as she had been the day before and again she was barefoot. He watched her as she approached across the great white rug. She looked very taut and cold.

"Well, Mr. Church?" she said in a chill, delicate voice.

"You lied to me, ma'am," he said bluntly.

She flushed. "What are you talking about?" she demanded.

"I'm talking about Mira Taliaferro."

When he said that the lady gazed up at him so intently for a moment that those gray-green eyes seemed to shoot sparks at him. Then she sank down slowly on the couch.

"How did you find out?" she asked after a moment.

"I gained entrance to her apartment and found her birth certificate," he told her. And now he understood her tears of the day before. Tears were trembling on her lashes now.

"All right," she agreed. "I lied. She happens to be my oldest daughter. But everything else I told you about her is true."

"Including your statement that you have no idea where she is?"

"Yes. I have no idea."

"You didn't know she had an apartment here?"

"I thought she was staying at The Sands."

"I have evidence," he went on, "that she was here in town as recently as Monday night."

Mrs. Taliaferro shook her head. "I've told you all I know."

He seated himself in the chair opposite her and when she finished dabbing at her eyes and looked at him he shook his head. "Not quite, I think," he said.

"Mr. Church," she advised him sharply, "whatever I have told you has been purely voluntary. I don't have to talk to you, you know. You want to find out where she is. I've told you I don't know. And now may I suggest you stop wasting your time and your client's money and go back to San Francisco."

He was ready for that. "How would you like to see a warrant out for her arrest?" he asked.

The lady's eyes blazed suddenly with cold green fire. "She hasn't done anything wrong!" she said. "Some love-sick fool of a man gave her a ring and a car. Now why, and on what grounds, would he get a warrant for her? You said yourself he didn't want to cause her trouble."

"He might change his mind," he said.

"He *gave* the ring and the car to her!"

"Gave them to her on the basis of a verbal understanding between them," he corrected. "She agreed to marry him. He would never have given her a valuable ring that belongs in his family unless there was the understanding that she would marry him and become a member of the family."

"Well—" Mrs. Taliaferro paused, shrugged and got her cigarettes out of her purse. She lowered her lashes as she leaned forward to meet the flame of his lighter. "In any event," she went on, exhaling, "they'd have to find her first."

He was silent a moment, gazing at her, then he said, "I can see how you'd lie to me, the young lady being the way she is.

You've got two other girls and you want to protect their good name. But I don't quite understand your present relationship with your daughter Mira."

"And I don't see any reason I should explain it to you," she said tartly. "You are threatening her with legal action, and while I don't condone her behavior, I frankly can't see that she has done anything criminally wrong."

Well, he thought, she lied to me, so I can lie. "Look," he told her, "let's put our cards face up. Frankly, I want to get back to San Francisco. I don't care if I find the lady or not, but I've got to have a plausible story to tell my client."

"There's nothing implausible in what I've told you," she said. Her manner and voice had abruptly changed. She wasn't so salty now.

"Maybe you didn't start far enough back," he suggested. He was thinking of that photograph again. "She was all grown and already taking the boys in your story yesterday," he said.

Mrs. Taliaferro regarded him steadily for a moment. Then she gazed out the windows at the blue sky, yet it was clear she was not really looking at the sky. She was looking back into the past, he thought, and what she saw there hurt. Her face did not soften, it hardened.

"All right," she said. "I'll begin right at the beginning."

The summer after her freshman year in college, she told him, she had gone to Europe with some other girls and at Monte Carlo she had met and fallen in love with a young Italian nobleman, the Count Carlo Solis de Taliaferro. She had married Taliaferro that fall and Mira had been their first child, born the following year in Rome.

"There was always a quality about Mira I can't describe," she said. She gazed at him. "The word I want to say is 'enchanted.' It was as if the child were enchanted. One felt that."

When Mira was sixteen, she continued, it was found she had tuberculosis and they had sent her to a sanatorium in Switzerland where, after a year of treatment, she had improved enough to be released. Shortly after her release she had run off and married a young American named Cheever. Her gay life with Cheever had landed her in the sanatorium again shortly after their marriage and while she was there Cheever had taken up with another woman and had asked for a divorce.

Mrs. Taliaferro shook her head. "Mira never recovered from that," she said. "From Cheever. After that her life took on the pattern I've told you of. Even us—her own family—she treats as strangers. Mira wants no lasting ties with anyone, any more—no friends."

While the lady talked Johnny had taken his notebook out and made a note or two. "Phone Whitney, the husband, in Chicago," he wrote now. He should have done that before, he knew.

"Well," Mrs. Taliaferro said abruptly, rising from the couch, "I guess that's about it, Mr. Church."

He also rose, but he had no intention of leaving. "I do have a few questions," he told her.

She gazed up at him for a moment. "All right," she agreed. And now it was clear to him that she was very nervous. Yet he had the feeling he was not the cause of her nervousness, but was only contributing to it. "Let's go out by the pool," she suggested. "I usually get some sun at this time of day."

He followed her out through the tall white doors to the pool and they sat down at an umbrella table. She leaned back with her face in the sun.

"You didn't know she was here getting a divorce, then?" he said. "I mean, that isn't the reason you came here?"

"No," she said. Her eyes were closed. "I told you—I'm here because I like to gamble. We met just as I told you, at the roulette table. I didn't know she had remarried until I talked to her."

"You wouldn't know anything about this Whitney that she came here to divorce, then?"

"No," she said.

At that point there was the sound of a car stopping outside. He heard the front door of the house flung open, then voices.

"The girls—" murmured Mrs. Taliaferro. She opened her eyes and looked at him. "Really, Mr. Church, I'm afraid there's absolutely nothing else I can tell you."

"There are a few more things," he said doggedly. And he had the queerest feeling now. He felt as if *she* were there somewhere— Mira. Or as if she had just left, trailing behind her that haunting, unforgettable scent. Then the twins appeared, claiming his entire attention, the two lovelies he had glimpsed by the poolside the day before. They were no longer clad only in nature's simple buff, to be sure, yet were still compelling to the eye dressed for tennis, in brief shorts, blouses and sneakers.

The two were of a size, of a shape, of an equal, though not of an entirely identical beauty and their eyes and the outlines of their lovely faces were instantly familiar, for they had the same fine bone structure as that face in the photograph, the same as their mother. They wore their hair in short, fluffy curls and the hair of one was chestnut colored, the other was an almond blonde. And, like their mother, these shapely creatures too had a splendid dignity about them. But with them there was no accompanying aura of chilliness. If the mother packed a charge, he thought, this duet of sibling sex bombs squared it. Their eyes focused on him hungrily, as if triangulating the range on a ship they intended without delay to sink.

He rose, gazing upon them and Mrs. Taliaferro introduced him. "Girls," she said with absolutely no enthusiasm, "this is Mr. Church. He's the detective who was here yesterday. He knows about our Mira now. Mr. Church," she continued, "these are my daughters. Lucerne—"

The one with the almond hair smiled at him. "Lu, please," she said.

"And Lausanne," said Mrs. Taliaferro.

The twin with the chestnut hair said, "Anne, please."

"They never did care for their names," Mrs. Taliaferro remarked. "As you might gather, I gave birth to them in Switzerland."

"Delighted to meet you," John Church told the young ladies.

"Now," Mrs. Taliaferro said to them, "go get out of those tennis things, girls. And rest a while before lunch today."

As the twins dutifully departed, a door in the wall on the far side of the pool opened and the man in the beret, who had evidently let the girls out at the front door and then driven the car around to the garage, stepped through and shut the door behind him. He was carrying a plastic bag full of tennis balls and three tennis rackets. He also wore sneakers. He glanced at Johnny, gave Mrs. Taliaferro a quick, appraising look and went on toward the rear part of the house.

Johnny sat down again. "Is your husband here with you, ma'am?"

"Heavens no!" Mrs. Taliaferro exclaimed. "I've been divorced many years. If you're wondering who that was who just came through that door, it's Sig, my driver."

"Someone you hired here in Las Vegas?" he asked.

"No," she declared with an air of fractured patience. "Sig has been with me a long time." She faced him. "Really, Mr. Church—" She paused as there was the sound of a phone ringing in the house. Then when the ringing abruptly ceased, she went on. "Really," she said, "I can't see the relevance of these questions."

He thought then she was going to suggest that he leave, but the maid appeared and called to her, "Telephone, ma'am."

"Excuse me," the lady told him shortly. She strode off across the flagstones into the house.

The moment their mother vanished the twins reappeared. They wore white Bikinis, token garments which seemed really more revealing than simple nudity.

They could be seventeen or eighteen, he thought, or they could be in their early twenties. Their disciplined expressions—except for that hungry flicker in their eyes—their perfect poise, the ripe beauty of their bodies, all hinted at the more advanced age. Yet there was a childish quality about them that puzzled him, a captive, repressed air. As they approached him he got the impression that they were like two prisoners seizing an opportunity for a moment's escape into the outside world.

He started to rise, but Anne, the one with the chestnut curls said, "Oh, please don't get up, Mr. Church."

They stood silently for a moment, smiling at him, examining him. Then Lu, the blonde one said, "You've come because of some man Mira met here in Las Vegas, haven't you? He's trying to find her."

"That's right," he said.

"Did he really fall in love with her?" Anne asked him.

He nodded. "That's the impression I got."

"They always do," Lu said. "She gold-digs them, makes fools of them, then she vanishes."

He took out his cigarettes and offered them to the girls, but they shook their heads. "We don't smoke," Anne said.

"We're not allowed to," said Lu.

He lit a cigarette and he realized that, though they spoke quite matter-of-factly, there was a hint of rebellion in their voices. "Did you see your sister while she was here?" he asked. Then, as they slowly shook their heads once more, he asked another question. "When did you last see her?"

As he watched them now he saw them change. Though standing there, flawless creatures in the brilliant sunlight, it was as if his words had cast a shadow upon them. Their eyes appeared suddenly to be haunted by old memories, by tragic, disenchanted thoughts.

"It's been a long time," Anne said finally.

"Where was it?" he asked.

They gazed at him, then they glanced beyond him and suddenly they turned and in tandem dived into the pool.

"Girls!" Mrs. Taliaferro called angrily behind him. "I thought I told you to rest!"

The twins' heads popped up from the water and they swam to the other end of the pool. Then the amber bodies appeared to flow up out of the pool and the two stood leaning over, shaking the water from their curls.

"Girls!"

"We're *going* to rest, Mother," one of them told her.

"We just wanted to take a dip and cool off," the other said.

Johnny rose and faced Mrs. Taliaferro. "They're great," he said. "I'd think with those two around this place would be crawling with guys."

"Thank you," Mrs. Taliaferro told him curtly, and as she spoke they could hear the phone start ringing again. "Mr. Church," the lady went on, "I want you to tell your client that I deeply regret what happened and I hope, as her mother, he will try to understand her and forgive her. You can tell him the whole sad story now."

"Can I?" he asked. He gazed at her and slowly shook his head.

"What do you mean?" she demanded.

Now he noticed the maid coming through the opened doors of the living room. She was looking at him. "You're Mr. Church, aren't you?" the maid asked him.

"Yes," he said.

"Somebody wants to talk to you on the phone."

He glanced back at Mrs. Taliaferro. "I gave a friend this number, told him I'd be here a while," he said. "All right if I take the call, ma'am?"

"Of course," she snapped.

He went into the living room and followed the maid into a wide, tiled hallway between the dining room and the living room, where the telephone was. He thanked the girl, sat down in a basket chair and picked up the instrument.

"Church here," he said.

"A guy just phoned me," Mitch Barry told him. "He wants the money tonight."

"What did you say?"

"I tried a bluff," Barry said. "I told him I didn't care if they printed that picture or not."

"Now you're getting smart," Johnny told him.

"Yeah? Well, listen. He tells me, 'You get that money up by tonight or we won't just print the picture. Somebody you like a lot will be dead.' I said, 'Who?' He says, 'Could be you.' "

"So?" Johnny asked.

"So I told him to call me back in an hour, then I hung up."

"I'll be around to see you in a little while," Johnny told him.

He put down the phone and watched the maid, who was putting place mats on the dining-room table and at the same time watching him. He smiled at her. "What's your name?" he asked her.

She moved over to the doorway. "Letty, Letty Clark," she said.

"What time do you get finished around here at night, Letty?" He kept his voice down so that she would too.

"Depends on when they eat at night," she told him in a whisper. "I'm through as soon as I clear up the dishes. Then unless Sig drives me back to town I got to walk down and get the bus."

"You don't sleep here, then?"

She shook her head. "They got a nice room and bath for a maid too."

"How about the cook?"

"Sig does the cooking," she said. "He cooks and drives and shops. He takes those twins around and does just about everything else. He's just like a slave to that lady."

"Mrs. Taliaferro?"

She nodded.

"Letty," he said quickly, "have you seen another young lady around here, a black-haired one?"

"No," she said. "I haven't seen anybody around here except them and you."

"Is it possible somebody else could be here?" he asked her. "Do you go into all the rooms?"

"I don't go into the twins' wing," she said. "Mrs. Taliaferro told me I wasn't ever to go in there and do anything for them because she had trained them to do for themselves."

"That's correct," a cold, furious voice said. It was Mrs. Taliaferro's voice.

Johnny turned and saw her standing behind him just inside the entrance to the living room and out of sight of the maid. How long she had been there was anybody's guess. Now she came soundlessly into the hall in her bare feet.

"Just *what* is in your mind, Mr. Church?" she asked him. "Do you think Mira may be *here*—in this house?"

He got up. "The idea did cross my mind," he admitted.

"Then you don't believe a word I've told you! I have wasted my breath talking to you."

"I didn't say that," he said.

"Would you like to *search* the house?" she asked. "Would that make you feel better?"

"It might," he agreed.

"And afterward will you please go away and leave us alone!"

He nodded. "Yes, ma'am."

"Very well," she said. "Where would you like to start?"

"The twins' wing, if you don't mind," he told her, but as she swung around and started off across the living room with him in tow, he felt he was wasting his time.

Since she was offering to let him make the search he was pretty certain he wasn't going to find anything.

CHAPTER SIX

O N THE OTHER SIDE of the living room Mrs. Taliaferro opened a door and he saw another tiled hall with a glass-brick wall on the left side facing on the court at the front of the house. On the right of the hall were the twins' bedrooms. The doors were open and from the first room there came a sound of music, a Count Basie recording.

"Girls," Mrs. Taliaferro announced, stopping at the doorway, "Mr. Church is coming in."

The twins, in terrycloth robes, were curled like kittens on the floor, a portable record-player between them. As he entered they gazed up at him with wide, surprised eyes.

"Turn that record off," Mrs. Taliaferro directed, and one of them promptly obeyed.

In the silence Johnny gazed about him and, though the room was feminine, it was also rather austere. The only scent he could discern was the faint, pleasant one of bath powder.

He glanced through the opened door of a closet; then he looked down at the twins and grinned. He was beginning to feel somewhat ridiculous.

"You haven't looked under the bed," Mrs. Taliaferro told him. "And aren't you going to open the bureau drawers?"

"No, ma'am," he said. There was a door that opened into a large, lavender-tiled bath and he could see across the bath into another bedroom.

"This is Lucerne's room," said Mrs. Taliaferro. "If you're convinced there's no one hiding here, we'll have a look at Lausanne's."

As she spoke she started through the bath into the other bedroom, and he almost told her to skip it. But by the time he could have spoken she was already in the other room waiting for him.

The other room, though the color scheme had been varied, was the same as the first. There was the same closet with its rack of clothes and luggage piled on the shelf above. There were the same chairs, bed, bureau-chest, writing desk, and yet there was a difference. For some reason he could sense *her* presence in that room.

He stood there, all his senses quickening. What was it? Was it only a hunch, he wondered, or was there some subtle but tangible reason for the feeling he had?

He moved around the room slowly, staring at things, not really knowing what he looked for. For a time he gazed at the items on the bureau—the traveling clock, a bottle of lotion, a box of tissues, a bracelet, a scarf. Next he moved over to the writing desk. There was a book lying face-down on the desk—poems. Then it was as if some force tugged gently at the corners of his eyes and he found himself gazing down into the wastebasket beside the desk. In the bottom of the wastebasket, beside a crumpled sheet of stationery, lay the butt of a gold-tipped cigarette.

After a moment he bent and picked the butt out of the wastebasket. He held it up between a thumb and forefinger, saw the smudge of lipstick on it. Then his eyes met Mrs. Taliaferro's.

"I didn't think your girls smoked," he said.

"They don't," she declared quickly. "That happens to be one of mine."

She was so smooth, he thought. Her expression told him nothing, yet he could feel shock waves of alarm coming from her. "I haven't noticed you smoking this kind," he observed.

"I don't usually," she said. "They're hard to get. They're Egyptian. Are you quite through, Mr. Church?"

He nodded. "I found what I wanted, ma'am. Now I'd like to tell you something." He gazed at her. "Not here, please."

She turned and he dropped the butt of the gold-tipped cigarette into his jacket pocket and followed her out. They went down the hall to the living room where she shut the door of the twins' wing. Then she turned and faced him.

"Tell me *what?*" she asked challengingly.

Now as he looked at her his battered ribs seemed suddenly to throb. He felt the fists again, and some of his fury of the night before returned.

"Listen," he told her. "She was *here*—maybe just last night. Those gold-tipped jobs are the cigarettes she smokes. Lady, I'm going to level with you. If you don't produce her I'm going to make trouble, not just because of the bunko job on my client, but for another reason. *She's* in trouble, lady. She's right in the middle of a blackmail job." He stared at her. "You heard that word?"

One of her hands moved spasmodically, fluttered and came to rest uncertainly against her lips. For an instant her face looked old, harried, desperate.

"If you don't produce her," he went on, "I'll go to the D.A. I mean that. There'll be cops here. They'll drag you in and question you. You'll get your name in the papers—"

"No!" she exclaimed. "It isn't *true!*"

"You want that?" he demanded.

She shook her head. "You're lying!"

"No," he told her, "that's your department." Then, glancing beyond her, he saw that character in the beret, Sig. He had come to the entrance of the hall where the telephone was. He was wearing an apron and holding a big kitchen knife and he was looking at John Church as if he would like to carve him.

"I'm not threatening you," Johnny told Mrs. Taliaferro. "I'm telling you. I'll be back here tomorrow about the same time of day and if I don't meet the young lady at that time you get cops." He gazed at her a moment, then he turned and strode out through the entry and left the house.

And it wasn't any bluff. At the time, at least, he meant it. He had been taken by a story, the ten year-old photograph of an enchanted face, a haunting perfume. He had been almost as bad as his client and all the rest, he thought, and *he* had never even met the young lady. But now he felt it almost a public duty to turn her in. Either that or turn in his license. She was, he decided, as dangerous in her way as any Typhoid Mary.

But then he thought, Who's to bring the charges? And he also thought, Really all that ails you, John Church, is that you want to *see* her!

CHAPTER SEVEN

ONE OF MITCH BARRY'S ROD BOYS was sitting in a car outside the singer's cottage on the grounds of the Nevada Grande reading a comic book when Johnny drove up. But when Barry came to the door in response to the bell he was alone. He was wearing pajamas, his bronze hair was mussed, he hadn't shaved yet and he looked as if he needed a sedative. He let Johnny in and went back to the couch where he had a cigarette burning and a cup of coffee.

Johnny sat down in the chair where he had sat the night before. His mind had been working in the car; it was still working. And when Barry started to talk he cut him off. He held up a hand and said, "Let me cogitate just a moment."

In reviewing all he had heard by now about the missing Mira there was nothing to suggest that blackmail had ever entered into her one-woman campaign to fleece the male population. That was the big question as he saw it—whether she had or had not been an accomplice in the case. Even if Mrs. Taliaferro produced her tomorrow, the question wasn't going to be answered. If she *was* a blackmailer, or a blackmailer's moll, she wouldn't be likely to tell him about it. Meanwhile a portrait had been painted and a touching one it was. You sympathized with this doomed and lovely lady, who had been so cruelly hurt by a man and who now, in her frenetic moments of living, spent her time—and, incidentally, financed herself—by getting even with men.

With this lady you sympathized, you understood, even forgave. You could see how none of her victims would wish to press charges against her. And all of them could afford what she took them for. But blackmail was different. Blackmail was a really nasty word.

One way or another, he decided—that is, whether Mrs. Taliaferro produced her tragic wayward daughter or not—he was going to have to go along with Mitch Barry. He had to find out whether she had been in that bed knowingly, as a principal in a vicious little drama, or whether she had been innocent of any but her own by now familiar designs.

And he knew he had to find this out not only to do complete justice in his report to his client. He knew he had to find out for his own sweet self.

He glanced over at Barry now. "How much time have we?" he asked him. "I mean till they phone you back?"

Barry looked at his watch. "About half an hour."

"Do you mind if I make a long-distance call?" he asked. "I'll pay you for it."

"You mean in connection with this case?" Barry said.

"Yes," he said.

"Go ahead," Barry told him. "But I'd like to know this right now. Are you working for me or aren't you."

Johnny got out his notebook. "I'm working for you," he said.

"How much will it cost me?" Barry asked.

"A two-hundred-and-fifty retainer right now," Johnny told him. "Make out the check to Gerard Secret Service, please." In his notebook he found the Chicago address he had gotten for Alan K. Whitney, then he picked up the phone and asked the girl on the Nevada Grande switchboard for long distance.

"Sure thing, honey," the girl said.

He got Whitney on the line in a matter of minutes. "My name is Church," he said. "I'm a private investigator. I'm looking for your wife, Mr. Whitney. She was here in Las Vegas, as you know, to establish residence to get a divorce from you. Now she's vanished."

"Vanished!" the Chicago voice said.

"Do you have any idea where I might locate her?"

"No!" Whitney said. "I was going to fly out there. I have written her, in care of her lawyer, but she's never answered my letters. I've wired her almost every day, tried to phone her. Even her lawyer won't speak to me. Do you know her address?"

"Yes," Johnny said, "but she's not at it. Would you answer a few questions, Mr. Whitney?"

"If I can," the man said. He sounded fairly frantic.

"How long did you know her?"

"About a week," Whitney said.

"How long were you married? I mean, how long did you live together as man and wife?"

"Well—" The man hesitated. "We were together one day—or night rather, after we got married," he said. "But actually, you see, we—ah—never were, if you know what I mean, man and wife. That's the point, Mr.—"

"Church."

"Mr. Church. You see, my children—I have a couple of grown children—threatened to take legal action to declare me incompetent if I allowed the settlement I made on her to go through."

"How much?" Johnny asked him.

"A hundred thousand dollars," Whitney said. "I signed a paper. I agreed to settle a hundred thousand dollars on her after she married me regardless of what happened. She married me; then she vanished. The next thing I knew I was served with a demand for payment of the settlement and, along with it, notice that she was suing me for divorce out there."

"Now you're contesting the settlement?" Johnny said. "Is that it? You won't pay."

"Under the circumstances," Whitney said, "I can't help myself. My lawyers and my children won't let me pay. I don't want to hurt her, Mr. Church. I'd *like* her to have the money, but the superior court here has approved an action to annul the marriage and set aside the settlement."

"So the divorce is off and she gets no money."

"That's right," Whitney said sadly.

"Do you know her mother?" Johnny asked him.

"I don't know anything about her family," Whitney said. "She never would speak of that sort of thing. Mr. Church, you say you're looking for her?"

"Yes, I am," Johnny told him.

"Would you find her for *me?* Will you tell her I've got to see her, talk to her?"

"You mean you want to hire me?" Johnny asked.

"Yes," Whitney said.

"There will be a two-hundred-and-fifty-dollar retainer," Johnny informed him. He told him how to make out the check and where to send it and he promised to report as soon as there was anything to report. Then he hung up.

Mitch Barry handed him the check he had made out and after Johnny put the check in his wallet he fished the gold-tipped cigarette butt from his pocket. "This look familiar?" he asked Barry.

Barry gazed at the cigarette butt. "It's one of hers," he said softly. "Where did you find it?"

"We'll go into that later," Johnny told him. "Right now we need a little rehearsal on what you're going to say when you get that telephone call." He glanced around. "Is there an extension on this phone?"

"In the bedroom," Barry said.

Johnny got up and went into the bedroom. The extension had a cord long enough so that he could sit in a chair in the bedroom doorway with the phone and, when the living-room phone was carried to the end of its cord the two phones would be only a few feet apart.

"As you may gather," he told Barry, "I'm going to listen in when you talk. If you see me put my hand over the transmitter you do likewise. It will mean I want to tell you what to say." He sat down in the chair with the extension phone.

"I want to catch this party," he said. "So we won't go for any drops. You've got to get him to agree to meet you and exchange that photo for the dough. You tell him you can't get up the fifty. Tell him, say, you've got twenty."

"I haven't got twenty," Barry said. "Contrary to what most people think, I'm broke."

Johnny said, "You're going to pay *nothing*. Get that clear. We're only going to try and set a trap."

"Suppose the trap doesn't work?" Barry said. "Then they bump me off!"

"Nah," Johnny told him scornfully. "That's just scare stuff. What would be the percentage? You're worth nothing to them dead."

As he spoke the phone rang and Barry jumped nervously. Then he sat down on the arm of the couch and stared at Johnny.

"Okay," Johnny said. "Now, listen, don't let them push you around. Talk tough." He nodded. "Go ahead," he said. And at the same instant that Barry lifted his phone from the cradle, he picked up the extension.

"Hello," Barry said.

"Barry?" The man's voice sounded thick and disguised.

"Yes," said Barry.

"You got it up?" the voice asked.

Barry said, "Some. I can't raise any fifty."

"How much you got?"

"Twenty."

"That's not enough."

Barry glanced at Johnny. "I can't do better," he said.

"You want to live?"

Johnny put his hand over the transmitter and Barry did likewise. "Ask him if he wants you to call the cops."

He listened while Barry repeated this over the phone.

"Don't mention cops to me," the voice said, "or you *will* get it. Understand? You get cute we'll really maul you."

Barry was sweating. "How do I know I can trust you?" he said. "How do I know you won't hold back a print of that picture?"

"If you don't try anything cute, we won't," the man said. "Wait a minute." For a moment there was silence and they knew he must have put a hand over the mouth-piece to talk to someone else. Then he said abruptly, "Look, be sure that twenty is in small bills and be waiting by your telephone at nine o'clock tonight with a map of Las Vegas on your lap." The voice stopped and the line went dead.

Johnny put down the extension and got up. He stretched, watching Barry, thinking it over. "Relax," he said to Barry.

"Sure!" Barry declared explosively. He stood up and reached for his cigarettes and when he lit one the hand that held the match developed a sudden tremor.

"I mean it," Johnny told him. "I'll handle it. All you have to do is be ready to talk over that phone at nine o'clock."

"I'll never be able to go on for my nine-thirty show," Barry said.

Johnny nodded. "You will," he said. "Look, you've retained me. Now maybe I can ease your mind a little. I think you could go to the D.A. with what you've got and *not* drag her in. You could decline to identify the lady. The D.A. could serve notice on that certain magazine that the minute anybody offered them a picture of that nature involving you they were to tip him off and cooperate in apprehending the vendor. If they bought the picture with the intention of printing it or writing a story about it he could charge them with being an accessory to blackmail."

"Then why all the hanky-panky with this guy over the phone?" Barry demanded.

"Because I think *she's* mixed up in it," Johnny said. "That's why. I want to try and find out."

"I tell you, you're nuts!" Barry exclaimed. "Why do you *think* that?"

"Think over one thing," Johnny told him slowly. "Why did they cut the faces out of that picture?" He shrugged and moved toward the door. "You sit tight for now," he said. "We'll at least see what the guy has to say tonight." He opened the door then and went out.

He didn't now how valid what he had said about going to the D.A. was. But *if* he couldn't catch himself a blackmailer who would lead him to her, and, *if* her mother didn't produce her, or tell him where she was, he decided it would, in the interests of client Barry, at least, be the best thing to do.

CHAPTER EIGHT

EMERGING FROM THE GROUNDS of the Nevada Grande he drove along The Strip to his motel. He parked outside his room, entered warily, after his experience the night before, and crossed to the luggage stand where his bag was. He opened the bag and took out his binoculars. Then he went back out to his car and drove along to Flamingo Road and turned east there toward Heavenly Knoll.

In a still undeveloped area, a pristine desert waste south and east of the knoll, there were other undulations in the land. The highest of them was a rocky butte where the geometrical pattern of development roadwork ceased and an aimless track meandered off through the sage and thorn to round the butte on its way to connection with some distant arterial.

When he had driven behind the butte he parked and got out of the car. There was a lovers-lane litter there—crumpled cigarette packages, empty bottles—and there was a path leading up the butte. He passed a torn brassiere, a contraceptive, lying like a shed snake's skin in the sun. Blue-bottle flies were droning around a mound of horse dung.

From the butte-top, seated on a rock he could see the pink house on Heavenly Knoll. He could see the garage with that pale blue station wagon in it, the wall around the swimming pool and the tops of windows beyond the wall. But he could not see the entrance to the house.

He leaned back with the binoculars in his lap, waiting, for what he did not know. And now there was the distant wailing of a fire engine in the town. There were vapor trails in the sky and after a while the droning of the flies became a hypnotic that made his eyelids droop.

He dozed, he knew, dreamed again of that enchanted face, yet still he did not quite sleep. Some senses remained sentinel enough to snap him awake at the remote sound of a motor starting.

It was the station wagon at the pink house and the sound of its starting was concentrated and magnified by the garage walls. Picking up the binoculars he saw the man Sig at the wheel, the maid on the seat beside him. He watched the car come roaring out, round the drive with a splatter of gravel. He heard it stop in front of the house. He got up then and ran back down the path to his car.

They had picked up Mrs. Taliaferro at the front door. He could see her sitting in the seat behind them as the station wagon went along Flamingo toward The Strip. Keeping a maximum distance, with cars between, he saw them turn north on The Strip toward town.

At the corner of Main and Fremont the maid got out and as the station wagon turned right on Fremont he speeded up. He made a right turn too and slowed, and as Letty came clipping and bouncing along on her high-heeled slippers he gave her the horn. She recognized him, gave him an eager-eyed look and a wave and he stopped and opened the car door for her.

"Where they going?" he asked her when she got in. Then he swore. Traffic had speeded up and he could no longer see the station wagon.

"I don't know where they're going," she said. "Maybe to find them a new maid."

"You quit?" he asked.

"She fired me," she said.

At the next corner he looked carefully up and down the cross street, but there was no pale blue station wagon in sight. He had, it would seem, been neatly ditched. "Do you think they knew I was following them?" he asked.

"If they did they didn't tell me," she said.

He drove on along Fremont. "What did she say when she fired you?"

"She let me wash the lunch dishes and finish cleaning up the house, then she told me she wouldn't need me any more. She said they would drop me in town. I was just going to walk along and go in places to see if they need a waitress maybe."

"Sure hope you connect," he said. He looked up and down the next cross street without seeing what he was looking for. Then he found a parking space and pulled into it. He gave the buxom young lady a cigarette and lit it for her. Then he lit one himself.

"What these people done?" she asked.

"Nothing I know of," he said. "The lady has another daughter, the black-haired one I asked you if you'd seen this noon. Her name is Mira. She's disappeared and I'm looking for her."

She shook her head, answering his question before it was asked. "I never heard them mention her."

"Who was it," he asked her, "who called Mrs. Taliaferro on the phone today while I was there?"

"Some man," she said. "He phoned her the day before too."

"Know his name?" he asked.

"No," she said.

"Did she get many calls?"

She shook her head. "Just that one man while I've been there. And the phone rang I think while I was washing dishes a while ago. I think I heard her talking on it. Then we left."

"How about the girls—Sig?"

"Nobody called them that I know of," she said.

He took a long, thoughtful drag on his cigarette. Mira, he thought. If thou art here, where art thou? Could it be that picture-taking had scared the delicate creature out of her wits? Could it be she was cowering under another name in some fleabag hotel? Or was she ill somewhere, perhaps dying!

"You don't think they were planning to leave town, do you?" he asked. "Did you see any signs of packing?"

"No," she said, "but they had a huddle after lunch. They all went into the twins' wing and shut the door. They were in there quite a while."

He had no more questions and when they finished their cigarettes he declared he had better be getting along, but he did write her telephone number in his notebook. He said to her as she got out, "When I wrap this up I'll ring you. We'll have a whirl, girl."

For a time after he let the maid out he combed the downtown streets, but he failed to find the station wagon. Then toward dusk, as an evening wind sprang up, he headed back out to the butte and when he had climbed once more to his vantage point among the rocks he saw that the station wagon had returned. Across the wind-swept waste its crystal eyes glowed palely at him from the shadows of the pink garage.

Just before dark he went back down the path to his car. He drove up Heavenly Knoll, parked near the house and got out. And that house was really designed for privacy. The only outside windows were the ones in the living room and below them the ground fell off so steeply that no one, unless he was flying a helicopter, could look in. All the other rooms opened on the pool area which, where it was not bounded by the house and garage, was enclosed by that ten-foot pink wall.

Through those living-room windows as he came along the drive only a faint light showed from somewhere else in the house. He went on into the front court and gumshoed up to the door. He put an ear to a panel and inside the house it was deathly still. Then abruptly there was a sound so wierd and strange that it made his flesh crawl. He didn't know what it was. At first he thought it was a woman sobbing. Then, as the sound died, he decided it could have been the wind moaning through an air conditioner or a kitchen ventilator.

He listened a while longer and heard nothing and finally he went away.

CHAPTER NINE

H E STOPPED at a place on The Strip and had a drink and a steak. Then he drove into a gas station, filled up the tank and got a Las Vegas map. By the time he parked in front of Mitch Barry's cottage at the Nevada Grande it was nearly nine o'clock.

Mitch Barry was there in the living room with his two goons. "Where the hell have you been?" he asked Johnny.

"Why," Johnny said mildly, "did something happen?"

"No," Barry said. "But we should be making some plans, shouldn't we?"

"We can't make any plans till we hear what the guy has to say." He stared at the two with the guns, the dark one and the blond one.

"You guys take a walk now," Barry suggested. "Stick around outside."

"No," Johnny told him, "let them stay here. They might as well be in on this. I figure we may need them." He took out his map and went in and sat in a chair with the extension, the way he had before. He spread the map out on the floor at his feet. Barry, he noticed, had a map on the couch.

Promptly at nine the phone rang. "You got the money ready?" that by-now familiar voice asked.

Johnny nodded and Barry said, "Yes."

"Okay, look at your map," the voice directed. "Find Black Mountain Road. You know it?"

"Yes," Barry said.

Black Mountain Road was about a mile south along The Strip. It ran west across the railroad tracks into the desert to connect eventually with Arville Road which angled down from the north.

"Go west along Black Mountain," the voice continued, "for three and a half miles. Check the mileage on your speedometer. After three and a half miles you'll come to a little side road on your left. Take that road for a mile, then turn off your lights, get out of your car and start walking straight ahead." The voice paused. "Got that?"

Johnny nodded at Barry. "I got it," Barry said.

"Then leave right now," the voice told him. "And if you know what's good for you, come alone. And don't try any tricks." The voice ceased. The line went dead.

Barry dropped the phone back on the cradle as if it were hot. He stared at Johnny. "Not me, pal!" he said. "I'm not going walking up that road alone."

Johnny rose. "No," he agreed. "You don't have to. Your pals can ride out there with me."

"And leave me here without anybody!" Barry exclaimed. "Oh, no. Take *one* of them."

"All right," Johnny said patiently. "One, then." He gazed at the pair. "Anybody volunteer?"

"What do we do out there?" It was the dark one who spoke.

"Till we see the set-up," Johnny told him, "we fly by the seat of our pants. The object, friend, is to nab these guys."

Neither of the two looked enthusiastic about the mission, but in their league "heart" was the thing. So while Johnny went over to the writing desk and stuffed some stationery into an envelop, they flipped a coin and the dark one got the assignment. He and Johnny went out and climbed into Mitch Barry's Cadillac and the dark one, who Mitch Barry called Merv, drove the car.

❦ ❦ ❦

There was no moon, and as they went west on the narrow black-top road the glare of The Strip faded in the sky behind them. Johnny could just make out the silhouette of the mountains against the stars ahead. He was keeping an eye on the speedometer and when they had gone three miles he said to Merv, "Slow it, boy."

A moment later the headlights picked out a dirt track running off to the south and Merv made a screeching, lurching turn. When the speedometer had clicked off a mile Johnny said, "Stop." Then he said, "Cut the motor and lights." And after that he sat there a moment with his eyes shut and when he opened them the blackness around the car did not seem quite so black. Still he could make out nothing much but the paleness of the road for a few yards ahead and the dark gray-green shapes of brush clumps near the car.

"What's next?" Merv said.

"Here's the money." Johnny dropped the envelope filled with stationery in his lap. "Now get out," he told him, "and start walking up the road."

"Me?" said Merv. "Why should *I* get out and walk up the God-damn road?"

"They must have cased the job good before they took that picture," Johnny explained. "You may not be Barry, but they know you're with him. *Me*—if they flashed a light on me they'd think he'd called in the cops for sure."

"What do I do after I walk up the road?"

"Do what they tell you to do. I'll be covering you all the way. And keep your hands at your sides. Don't go for that hardware of yours until the situation develops and you've absolutely got to go for it. Understand?"

"I understand, but that *don't* mean I like it," Merv said. He put a hand on the door handle. "When do we start?"

"Now," Johnny told him. He slid under the steering wheel and got out Merv's door, bumping into him. Then he shut the door and the sound was like a challenge flung into the black, looming silence of the night.

As Merv started walking up the road, Johnny moved over into the brush, groping his way forward on a course parallel to the road. His footsteps were muffled by the sandy desert loam and, though he could not hear the dark one walking, he could see his head moving against the stars. He could also make out the shape of his white sharkskin jacket. And now there was a blackness rising ahead that was more intense than the night itself and the pale stream of the road debauched suddenly into a large pale pool. Then a finger of light stabbed down from a black eminence and he saw the yawning mouth of an old mine shaft and a rocky ridge above it. The light from the ridge picked out a pile of rusted tin cans and the chassis of a wrecked car before it came to rest on Merv. He was pinned in its unblinking white stare.

"You're not Barry!" a voice called grimly.

"I'm Barry's pal," Mery answered. "I come for him."

There was a silence, then the voice said, "Don't move. If it's a trick you can get shot dead for Barry."

Johnny drew the Magnum and knelt behind a clump of sage as the light moved, coming to rest first on the car, then thoroughly exploring the perimeter of the desert floor in front of the ridge where the mine shaft was. Finally, the light returned to the area of littered sand where Merv stood, picked him out once more.

"Got the money?" the voice asked.

Merv held out the envelope. "Here," he said.

And by then, John Church was already gumshoeing cautiously through the brush once more.

"Take the money out of that envelope," the voice directed.

It was the same voice; he was certain. But now it appeared to come from a point several yards to the left of the light. He stopped, raised the Magnum and fired twice, and with his second shot the light went out and he started running toward the ridge. And now Merv was firing.

He shouted at him, "Hold it!" Then he ran on up the ridge to the left of the mine shaft and when he stopped to listen he could hear a crashing in the brush on the far side of the ridge, stones tumbling.

He went on to the top of the ridge. Then in the starlight he could see a road, he could see headlights, and he knew it must be the Arville Road, which the Black Mountain road ran into. He fired a couple of times, listened and fired again, then he yelled to Merv.

"Go back to the car," he told him. "See if the road we're on comes on up here."

The way he figured it, though, the road didn't. He figured they had been led into a cul-de-sac and, as he ran on, he saw he was right. He heard a car start up and go streaking off along the Arville Road. Then the lights pf the Cadillac burgeoned in the sky behind him and it was clear that there was no road over the ridge.

Merv drove up to the entrance of the mine shaft and banged the horn. The headlights of the car lit the ridge and when Johnny went back down toward the mine shaft he saw the big flashlight that had been wedged in a crevice between two rocks. His second slug had smashed the light but had not dislodged it from the crevice. He snapped on his own flashlight then and examined the footprints around the smashed light, but it was impossible to tell in the sand how many pairs of feet had made the prints.

CHAPTER TEN

H E TOOK THE WHEEL from Merv and he scorched the asphalt with that car of Barry's going back to the Strip. Then he took it as fast as he dared along Flamingo to Lariat Lane and up to that pink house on the knoll. When he swung past the garage of the house the Cadillac's head-lights picked up only emptiness in there. The station wagon was gone, which of course proved nothing at all. Yet, nevertheless it was of interest to him.

When they returned to the Nevada Grande, Barry was on. They could hear him singing as they approached the door of the supper room and, with his phrasing, Johnny thought, he could have made even rock-and-roll sound good. But he didn't linger there to listen. He kept thinking, What if they skipped? Merv could report to Barry.

"Keep your eyes on that thrush of yours tonight," he advised Merv. "It might just be they'd go to rough him up a little now, if they got the chance. Or maybe they'll phone again. If they do, tell him to let me know." He went out then and got in his car....

This time he parked behind a clump of sage on a side street at the foot of the knoll and walked up the road to the house. He passed the back door, which must, he guessed, open into the kitchen. There was no light on in there. In the living room, though, lamps were glowing through that big window above his head. But when he put his ear to a panel of the front door he could hear no sound inside, and the glass brick that formed the outer wall of the hallway in the twins' wing was dark. He tried the doorknob. The door was locked.

He went around to the garage then, flashed his light in there and saw the door that led to the quarters over the garage. But that door had a padlock on it and he didn't fool with it. The door that opened from the garage onto the pool terrace had a tough lock too, so he went out of the garage and on around to the kitchen. There he found he didn't have to pick a lock. The casement window was unfastened and in a minute he was in. He went through that window and made a three-point landing in a sink.

For a moment he listened, squatting there in the sink with his flashlight in his hand. But there was no sound save the ticking of a clock on the wall. He could see through a doorway into the dining room, see the light that flowed from the living room through the hallway where the telephone was reflected on the dining-room table.

He got out of the sink and moved silently across the tile to the doorway and, just as he reached it, the telephone burst into strident life, startling him so that he whipped out his gun.

Just from hearing that telephone, he thought, you would guess no one was there. It had that lonesome, hopeless sound, as if it had tried before and got no answer. Then, just when he thought it must stop ringing, he had to cross swiftly into the hall and pick it up, thinking, Who can be calling them? Perhaps *she's* waiting there at the other end of the line, listening to that empty ringing.

But when he lifted the instrument it was a man's voice he heard. "Hello," said the voice. "Hello? *Hello!*"

He broke the connection and moved into the living room and the ringing began once more as fast as someone could re-dial the number.

Had they blown town? There was nothing in the living room to indicate they hadn't, nothing at all in there of a personal nature. After looking through the empty drawers of a desk he crossed to the opened door that led into the twins' wing. Then, snapping on his flashlight, he relaxed. The record player was still on the floor of the first bedroom where it had been that noon and there were records, shoes and clothes strewn about the room.

They hadn't gone, at least not yet. Still he had a feeling of crisis hovering there, a feeling which the imperative, unanswered voice had abetted, a feeling of terminal events impending. And once more he sensed *her* there.

Neither she, or her aura, however, was in the twins' rooms and after he had flashed his light around he went out and recrossed the living room to the hall where the telephone was. Beyond the dining room and kitchen there was a bare little room opening off the hall which would, he decided, be for a maid. At the end of the hall were double doors and when he opened them and flashed his light inside he saw a large, feminine bedroom with French doors opening onto its own small, high-walled patio. And *she* was there, at least her scent was there.

That perfume he was never going to forget. To him it was the exotic lady he sought and always would be elusive, tantalizing, strange. He moved on into the room, noting as he did how his heart was hammering. For a moment he stood gazing through a dressing room into a cream-and-purple bathroom, then he noticed the opened box of gold-tipped cigarettes she smoked on the bedside table, one with her lipstick on it lying crumpled in an ashtray. And it must have been her body, he thought, that had made that impression on the bedspread, and on that mound of little pillows her head had surely rested while she lit that ciga-rette, only almost instantly to extinguish it. And now, as he stood there, there was the sound of a car. It was coming fast, sweeping up the knoll, its tires spinning gravel as it made the turn into the drive.

He was out of there as the car stopped in front of the house and was going through the kitchen door when the chimes sounded.

The car was a taxi. As he came around the corner of the garage he saw it. He heard the dispatcher's voice on the two-way radio and heard the driver reply. Then the voices ceased and the chimes in the house had stopped and in the stillness there was a small, metallic sound. Someone was trying a key in the front door.

He went on then, making no effort to minimize the sound of his footsteps on the gravel of the drive. He passed around the rear of the taxi and saw the man at the door in the glow that came from the light beside the door. The man had heard him and turned, was staring at him, without guilt or apprehension, with only an angry, aggressive curiosity.

"Who are you?" he asked Johnny.

"A friend of the family," Johnny said.

The man was short and dark, middle-aged, wearing a sharp dark suit and a cocoanut-straw hat. He was holding a bunch of keys. "Mrs. Taliaferro ain't here?" he demanded.

"No," Johnny said. "I've been waiting around for her."

"She ain't left town?"

Johnny said she hadn't. "Can I give her a message?" he asked.

"You can tell her Nick was here." The man dropped his keys in a coat pocket and started toward the taxi, moving with short, quick steps. He yanked the taxi door open and plunged in, slamming the door as the taxi spurted off.

"Okay, Mr. Nick," Johnny murmured, watching the tail lights vanish around the house. And he thought, Don't I know you? Then he realized it was probably only because he knew so many others like him, short and dark, with the heavy-lidded eyes and the authority of cash, however come by. These were men in whose background somewhere there would be a circular with their photograph on it and a placard with a number hung around their neck. But that was the past. In this place, in this time, they were legit.

After a moment he walked back down the knoll, got in his car and drove to his motel. When he checked at the desk for messages there were two. One was from his San Francisco client, Hamilton Sprague, the other from his Chicago client, Alan K. Whitney. And, since he hadn't told Whitney how to reach him, he gathered that Whitney must have phoned Gerard Secret Service in San Francisco to find out where he was staying. Both messages simply said, "Call me."

He went to his room then. He unlocked the door, kicked it inward and entered with drawn gun, but there were no visitors. And, among the many things that puzzled him, this day of freedom from assault did. Yesterday somebody had wanted him to get out of town with such fierce intensity that they had half-killed him to convince him of it. Today nobody seemed to care.

He phoned Hamilton Sprague first, told him the facts to date and bluntly suggested that from what the missing lady's mother had said, he was one of a succession of suckers and that it looked as if the lady might also be mixed up in a blackmail case. He said he expected to get some results the next day. Namely, he thought Mrs. Taliaferro knew where her daughter was and he figured he had scared her enough to produce her.

"Church!" Mr. Sprague yelled at him over the wire. "I don't believe it—that blackmail and stuff. It's all a damnable lie. Listen, I'm coming down there." He told Johnny to reserve a room for him where he was staying and said he would catch a plane in the morning.

Johnny called Mr. Whitney next and the reaction he got from him was identical to Sprague's. Whitney also declared he would catch a plane in the morning and asked Johnny to reserve him a room.

It did Johnny no good to tell them they could accomplish nothing by coming there. Just the mention of the missing lady's name, he realized, was like catnip to them. Now that they thought they might see her again wild horses could not restrain them.

As soon as the connection with Whitney was broken he gave the operator on the motel switchboard the number of the pink house and for a time he listened to the measured ringing, the bell voice shrilling in the empty house. Then he put the phone down and went out, got in his car once more and drove north along The Strip.

And presently, he once more stood at the back door of that apartment on Panamint Drive. Again he pried the lock and entered, this time with his flashlight in one hand, his gun in the other. He moved across the living room, came to the bedroom door within the magic realm of that now familiar scent, and in the beam of light he saw the empty dresser top, the opened, empty drawers and when he went on into the room he saw that the closet too was empty. Except for that lingering scent, no trace of her remained.

When he got back to Heavenly Acres there was a glow in the sky above the wall of the pool from the lights in the twins' windows. And there was a soft light filtering up from the little patio and also a light in the quarters above the garage.

He parked where he had before, at the foot of the knoll, and as he sat there smoking the lights went out, one by one. When he started the car and drove away he had the conviction she was up there now in that pink house.

CHAPTER ELEVEN

I T WAS OVERCAST in the morning and there was a dry little wind. The wind ruffled the sterile waters and plucked at the umbrellas on the pool-side tables. Wind and sky brought gloom to The Strip. And that pink house atop its knoll of landscaped sand looked spectral and monstrous in the cold gray light. Without the burning balm of sun, or night and neon, nothing in that garish desert complex seemed quite right.

Even the chimes, when he pressed the button, had a hollow, sepulchral sound. He waited a while, then sent the tinkling, downbeat summons echoing through the house again. And as the sound faded away the door was abruptly opened and he and the man Sig, in his beret, stood gazing at each other. Sig had an apron on. He held a tea towel and a knife and as he regarded Johnny with a black, unblinking stare he caressed the long blade of the knife slowly with the cloth.

"What you want?" he asked after a moment. And his voice, heard this first time, was basso and heavily accented. It was also flat and challenging.

Czech or Bulgar, Johnny thought. Middle Europe. Then he wondered by what strange chance he had come into the service of the Lady Taliaferro. He wondered too, as he stood there and looked him over, what everything this service or enslavement might entail.

"I want to see Mrs. Taliaferro," he said at last. "I have an appointment."

The man made no reply. He simply started to slam the door, but John Church had a foot in it. "Not so fast," he said, and his right hand had slipped up under his jacket. It was resting now on the butt of the Magnum, snug there against his hip.

The black eyes glittered in that cold and gloomy light, and for a moment the knife did too. Then the man stepped back and Johnny followed him into the living room, waited there while the squat, aproned figure vanished into the hall where the telephone was.

On the table in front of the sofa, where he had sat with Lady Whitebritches, there were now four long-stemmed glasses, dregs of pale liquid in them, and an opened bottle of champagne.

Four glasses, he thought. Somehow he could not see that Sig drinking out of one of them. But he could see the dark and bewitching Mira lifting a glass of the bubbly stuff. He could see the twins and the mother drinking a toast to the exotic prodigal's return.

She's here! he thought. They've taken the things from her apartment and brought her here.

And yet he had no impression of champagne happiness in that house. The gloom of the morning had followed him in, was deepening and steeping there. He sat down on the sofa and stared out at the shrouded vista of desert. Then he noticed how tracked and soiled the white rug was. They had been walking in sand. Some of the sand was rust colored, some almost black, and there were bits of brush.

About him now the house was utterly still, so still that after a time it seemed to throb with its own silence. And when he stamped his cigarette out in the ashtray, rattling the tray against the tabletop, the noise was like gunfire. He rose nervously then and strolled across the room, opened the tall white doors and stood staring out at the sullen gray face of the sky mirrored in the ruffled pool. Presently there was a whisper of sound behind him and when he turned he saw a woman coming toward him and at first, so changed was she, he did not recognize that it was Mrs. Taliaferro.

She was wearing a dressing gown of quilted black satin and she had no make-up on. Even her hair appeared to have lost its luster, her eyes all the life that had been in them, while beneath its tan her face was as gray as the day. She looked old, and her bloodless lips, he realized, were etched deep with grief.

Her appearance robbed him of speech. And there was no effort at amenities on her part. She came up to him, looked at him and through him, then said with stark simplicity, "You are too late, Mr. Church. My daughter Mira is dead."

He stared at her. "No!" he exclaimed after a moment. "I don't believe it!" Suddenly he wanted to seize her and shake her. What she said was just too outrageous.

She gave a shrug, as if to indicate her complete indifference to his reaction. Then she turned in an aimless, distracted way and started wandering off across the room.

He strode after her. "What is this!" he demanded. "What are you saying? *When* did she die? *Where?*"

Mrs. Taliaferro had stopped. She was gazing at the champagne bottle, the glasses. "When we came back we drank champagne, just as she asked us to," she said. "And we filled a glass for her and we all drank that." Her voice broke, he saw her shudder and when he moved around to stand before her he saw the tears rolling down her cheeks. "Oh, God bless her," she whispered.

"When you came back from *where?*"

"From burying her," she said. She moved forward a few uncertain steps and sank down on the sofa. "From *burying* her!" she repeated, and now a sob shook her.

Johnny seated himself on an arm of the sofa and watched her and when she appeared once more to have herself in some control he said, "Lady, what is all this? What are you trying to give me?"

She glanced over at him, as if just now noticing his presence in the room. "Nothing," she said.

"What's this *burying* business?"

She shook her head. "I don't know what you are talking about," she declared.

"You said that when you came back from *burying* her you drank that champagne!"

"Oh, did I?" she asked.

He stood up. "Well, in that case, I'm going to the D.A.," he said. "You can tell him all about it."

"Oh, yes," she said. "Do that, by all means. You've nothing else to do, have you? Nothing but to run around making trouble for helpless women, people already lost in tragedy and distress."

"If you'll tell me the truth," he said, "you'll have no trouble."

"You never believe me when I do tell you the truth," she said.

He stood gazing down at here. "*Where* did she die?" he asked after a moment.

"*Who?*" she asked.

He turned then and started for the front door. But as he did, the door to the twins' rooms opened and they came drifting listlessly in. They were wearing their white terry-cloth robes and, like their mother, they did not look so good. They had no make-up on, their eyes were swollen from crying and their pretty noses were red. He stopped and they gazed at him a moment without greeting him, then they moved toward their mother.

"Mr. Church," Mrs. Taliaferro called.

"Yes, ma'am," he said, turning.

"You've got to swear that you won't tell anyone," she said. "That you won't make trouble."

He went back then and stood in front of her. Now the twins had settled themselves on either side of her, Lu on her right, Anne on her left. "I can't swear to anything," he said, "until I know what I'm swearing to."

"I won't tell you unless you swear," she said.

"You could have committed a crime," he went on. "Murdered somebody. Maybe tried to *blackmail* somebody."

She shook her head. "No. Nothing like that."

"You haven't committed a crime or broken any laws, have you?"

"Well—technically perhaps," she said. "But I feel sure you will understand. Beneath your cold and businesslike exterior, Mr. Church, you must have a heart somewhere."

"It was the way she wanted it," Anne said. "We had to promise her."

"And so right for her," Lu said. "Any other way—" She stopped abruptly and exchanged a glance with her sister, then the two of them burst into tears.

Johnny moved back and sat down in a chair facing the couch, and suddenly he had a sick and terrible feeling. She *was* dead, he knew it now, and he felt robbed. He felt like bawling too. "*If* you didn't kill somebody—something really bad—" he said, "I'll swear." He would have sworn at that point to anything. He had to know. That face from the photograph was haunting him and would, he felt, the rest of his days.

For a long moment Mrs. Taliaferro gazed at him. Then she took a cigarette from the box on the table and lit it. "Mira phoned yesterday afternoon," she said abruptly. "Something had frightened her and she was afraid to stay in her apartment. She had been living under another name in a small hotel—just lying in a room with the blinds drawn—ill. She hadn't eaten for days and she had acquired a craving for some pistachio ice cream, she said. She had gone out to a drugstore, but they had no pistachio and she had felt too ill to look further. She wanted to know if we would get the ice cream for her, so we went to her, Sig and I. We found a place that sold the ice cream she wanted. Then we brought her here."

"That was when you drove the maid in to town?" he asked.

"It was," she said.

"Did you know I was following you?"

She nodded. "Sig saw you, Mr. Church. We couldn't have you barging in." She drew deeply on her cigarette and blew the smoke out, staring at it. "She was dying then," she said tonelessly. "I knew it even when she phoned."

And now, with the words, the twins released a sob in unison.

"You're telling me," he said, "that she died here in this house last night. Is that it?"

"Yesterday evening," Mrs. Taliaferro said. "About seven o'clock."

"Did you call a doctor?"

"No," she said. "She wouldn't have let me. And anyway, a doctor would have been of no use."

"Where is she now—the body?" he said. "What have you done with her?"

"We buried her," she said calmly. "Out in the desert. Last night."

"In the most beautiful, far-away spot," said Anne.

"It was what she wanted!" Lu told him intensely. "It was like her. Anything else would have been wrong, you see. If only you had known her you would understand."

"She made us *promise* to do it," Mrs. Taliaferro said, and now tears glistened in her empty, lusterless eyes. "We simply couldn't have *strangers* touching her, staring at her!" she wailed. "We simply couldn't give her over to all that ghastly, ghoulish routine of undertakers, death certificates, preachers—that ranting at the grave!"

For a time then the three of them wept, and during that time he sat there, watching them, staggered, speechless. Then finally, as their sobs subsided, he took a deep breath and said to Mrs. Taliaferro, "You are telling me, ma'am, that you just took her somewhere out in the desert in your car, dug a hole and buried her. Is that it?"

"Oh, no!" Mrs. Taliaferro exclaimed in an anguished voice. "No, no, no!"

Lu ran her hands slowly upward through her short, almond-blonde curls, staring at him, her eyes dark now with feeling. "We bought her the most beautiful little casket," she told him. "You just *have* to understand, Mr. Church! Everything about this was beautiful. There was the night, the stars, the lovely desert. The fragrance of the sage."

"And the gorgeous place we took her," Anne of the chestnut curls said. "A little canyon, with the rock all different colors, and wildflowers growing there."

"Where is this place?" he asked. And now, in his mind's eye, he was trying to visualize the scene—the four of them in the desert night, carrying a casket through the sand. And somehow he *could* visualize it. They were just the ones to do it.

"It's near a dude ranch where we used to go horseback riding," Lu told him. "North of here."

"How far?"

"It's about twenty-five miles," Anne said. "There's a crazy little road that runs over from the ranch into some interesting old hills where there are the weirdest-shaped rock formations you ever saw. It reminds you of the moon or something, like some other planet. And there's this canyon. It's off the road a ways. We discovered it one day and we got off our horses and just sat there for the longest time. It was so beautiful and strange."

"It was like being in a cathedral," Lu said. "Only better. Now, when we die, we're all going to be buried there with her. We have made a bargain on that. Haven't we, Mother?"

Mrs. Taliaferro nodded. She was gazing at Johnny. "You won't tell, will you?" she asked him. "You won't make trouble for us because we have done this thing?"

"No," he said. "*If* all this really took place the way you say I won't tell or make trouble for you. But, lady, I warn you, I am going to make very certain it *did* take place. I am going to check you all the way."

Mrs. Taliaferro gasped. "You mean you don't believe us!" she demanded incredulously.

"You have lied to me before," he reminded her.

"But how, in heaven's name, do you think we could ever make up such a story!" she wailed. "What on earth would be the purpose?"

"You have shown a great desire to get rid of me," he said. "You have wanted me to get out of town. You could figure this really ought to do it."

"I don't give a damn what you do!" the little lady snapped, and there was more weariness now in her voice, he thought, than anger. "It's a matter of complete indifference to me," she told him. "I'm only sorry at this moment that I ever gave you any information at all."

"You told me things only when you were trapped," he said. "Only by way of explaining why you told me lies." He stood up. "First of all," he now advised her, "I want to see that grave."

In the wake of his words a silence fell and in it mother and daughters exchanged glances. Then Mrs. Taliaferro shook her head. "No!" she exclaimed.

"You've got to give me some proof," he said. "Otherwise it's the D.A."

"Oh, stop threatening me with that man!" Mrs. Taliaferro cried distractedly. She jumped up and paced a moment, then stopped and stared at him. "You're a complete cad, aren't you?" she said.

"Look—" Lu told him. "It's just that the place is sort of *sacred* to us, don't you see?"

"Oh, don't waste your breath trying to appeal to him," Mrs. Taliaferro said. "He has no heart. Let him get his friend the D.A. Let them dig her up and put us all in jail!"

"Lady," he said, as the twins began to weep and wail again, "I *have* one, and, if what you tell me is true, you're breaking it. But I can't buy the story without proof."

Mrs. Taliaferro began to pace again. Presently she stopped at the big window and stood there staring out, then she turned. She looked at John Church and said, "All right! We'll give you proof. We'll drive you out there. Then, when you are convinced, will you go away and leave us alone? Will you *please* do that!"

He nodded. "I will," he said. "When I am convinced, ma'am, I will."

CHAPTER TWELVE

I T TOOK THE LADIES a long time to get ready to go. Meanwhile the weather did not improve. The afternoon was going to be worse than the morning. The sky was darker, the wind sharper. And it was amazing when the three Taliaferros reappeared how they could change themselves, by artifice and paint transmute dross female stuff to golden beauty. What they had done to themselves he did not know, but it gave him food for thought. They looked like three entirely different numbers than the tearful, grief-ravaged trio he had been talking to earlier. They were wearing pants, Capezios and sweaters, and once more Mrs. Taliaferro looked like the twins' sister.

It was she who drove, that exquisite little lady, with Johnny sitting on the front seat of the station wagon beside her, Lu and Anne occupying the seat behind. And now their eyes were clear and cold and bright, their hair like spun silk, and their faces were masks of contained tragedy.

In silence they sped north along The Strip, then they turned west on Charleston and took the Tonopah road, out past the airport into a lowering wilderness of rock and thorn.

"I love the desert," a voice remarked dreamily after a while.

For a moment he gazed at a cameo-like image in the rearview mirror, not really knowing which face he looked at because he could not see the hair. And now he realized there was a depth in these two, a common, subterranean self. They weren't just the transparent, perfect children by the poolside. That aspect of them seemed to him now almost a pose.

He turned. "Why?" he asked.

"Because," Anne said, "one sometimes sees such lovely mirages." She glanced at her sister. "Isn't it true?"

"True, dear," said Lu.

"Girls!" Mrs. Taliaferro said sharply.

He thought that over for a time, brooded over it. Something was plucking at his mind, but he could not isolate it, pin it down for what it was. Then he thought that what bothered him must have been the subconscious knowledge of another car, one that perhaps was following them. He became aware of the other car's behavior gradually, glancing at it in the mirror, seeing how it kept its distance far behind, how it hung there, steadily pacing them, too far away to identify.

After a while Mrs. Taliaferro turned on the radio, got first a hill-billy blare, next something classical. He didn't know what it was but it was as gloomy, as sad and as strange as the day.

"Rachmaninoff's Third!" exclaimed a voice behind him. "How *odd* they should play it now."

"How she used to love it," said the other. And their voices too had changed, he thought. They were more vibrant, exciting to hear.

About fifteen miles beyond the airport Mrs. Taliaferro turned off onto a branching, black-top road leading west. In the distance now there were low, cinnamon-colored hills. Ultimately, that other car also made the turn.

They went on to the west for five or six miles. Then, where the road bent north again along a dry creek and the buildings of the dude ranch could be glimpsed through a screen of willows, the lady turned on a dirt road that wound back through the hills.

Soon they were deep among the hills, and some of the weird rock formations that had been mentioned began to appear. It was quiet and ghostly back in there out of the wind, with big yellow owl eyes staring balefully from holes in the rock as they passed. As far as he could tell, the other car did not follow them along the dirt road.

To reach the canyon they had to get out of the car and walk up a trail. Then they came around a black, jutting shoulder of rock and there was a towering pocket, carved by ancient tides in the rock, an eerie, haunted place where the wind moaned among multi-colored spires. And the twins, moving with the grace of dancers, swept along to a spot where stones had been artfully arranged, wild flowers strewn, and there they fell to their knees, undulating and weeping.

How nutty can you get? he wondered in a drugged and absent way. And yet he was profoundly impressed. If this was indeed real and true, this scene he was witnessing, it seemed to him that everything else the Taliaferros had told him must also be true.

"This is where you buried her?" he asked Mrs. Taliaferro.

"There, where the girls are," the lady said. There were tears in her eyes.

"You had no difficulty carrying the casket?"

"No," she said.

"You dug the grave, then lowered the casket and covered it?"

"Yes."

"And how did you lower the casket into the grave?" he asked.

"Sig brought ropes," she said.

He had a couple of more questions, but he let them wait until they were on their way back to town. That car that had followed them out had parked among the willows near the ranch. He could see it loafing along on the horizon behind them when they made the turn onto the highway.

"Where did you buy the casket?" he asked Mrs. Taliaferro.

"Oh, heavens," she said, "I don't remember. Some undertaking place. I was in no condition to notice names or details."

"Could you tell me roughly where the place was?"

"It was on some side street," she said impatiently.

"You wouldn't remember which street?"

"No!" she declared. "What difference does it make?"

They rode on in silence for a time, then Anne said, "I can't remember the name of the place, either, Mr. Church, but I know it was near the hospital."

"Thank you," he said.

"And it was a side street," Lu told him.

"It was quite a new place," volunteered Mrs. Taliaferro. "If that means anything. And the man was so loathsomely unctuous! The thought of him touching *her* made me quite ill."

Again they rode in silence. Then he said, "I gather you got her key and took her things from the apartment on Panamint Drive?"

Mrs. T nodded. "Last night," she said. "On our way back."

"May I ask if you happened to find that emerald and diamond ring I told you about among her effects?"

"She gave it to me," Mrs. Taliaferro said. "She made me promise to pawn it or sell it to pay whatever expense we incurred in her burial."

"Did you?" he asked.

"Did I what?"

"Pawn the ring, or sell it?"

"I pawned it," she said.

"And would you happen to have the pawn ticket?"

"Pawn ticket?" she echoed blankly.

"Didn't you get a receipt of some kind when you pawned the ring?"

"Oh—"she said. She frowned. "I don't remember. I tell you, Mr. Church, can't you understand? She just *died* last night! We *did* all this last night. I was simply in no condition—"

"Why don't you look in your purse?" Anne suggested.

Lu leaned over the back of the seat and picked up her mother's purse. After a moment she replaced the purse and handed Johnny a pawn ticket.

"Thank you," he said. He glanced at Mrs. Taliaferro. "Would you allow me to turn this ticket over to my San Francisco client so that he can redeem his ring?" he asked.

She shrugged. They were back in the town now. They were in the traffic. "Go ahead," she said. "I have no use for it."

After that he did not speak to the ladies again until they all got out of the car in front of the pink house on Heavenly Knoll. Then he said to Mrs. Taliaferro that he was sorry that in the course of his work he had been obliged to bother her. He expressed his sympathy over the loss of her daughter and he promised not to reveal the clandestine burial. He then bid the twins good-by and got in his rented car and the three lovely ladies waved to him as he drove off down the knoll.

CHAPTER THIRTEEN

THE GILLESPIE FUNERAL HOME was on a side street near the hospital. And it was new—chrome, glass brick and plate glass—an airy, immaculate temple to mortality, with its own chapel, from which recorded organ music in muted volume drifted out through the rest of the establishment.

Gillespie's was, as both decor and personnel strove to indicate, the Home of the Friendly Funeral. On his entrance he was met by a beautifully groomed gray-haired lady in white who gave him a tender, friendly smile and said at once in a voice heavily larded with compassion, "Won't you please tell me how we may help you? I'm Beth Potter."

"You sell caskets?" he asked her.

"We do *everything*," she whispered soothingly. "You can just let Gillespie take over right from this moment until the interment." She paused. "Your wife?"

"No," he said. "I just want—"

"A parent?" Her eyes showed pain. "Not your *mother*, was it, dear?"

"I just want to talk to the man who sells the caskets," he told her.

"Of course," she agreed. "You understand all Gillespie package plans include casket. And now one moment, please. Your name?"

"Church."

"Won't you please be seated, Mr. Church?" She retreated behind a white arc of desk and flipped the switch on an intercom.

"Mr. Gillespie," she said, as reverently as if she were talking on a private line with God, "Mr. Church is here."

Johnny had just sunk deep in a chair that appeared to sigh and wrap foam-rubber arms soothingly about him when a plump, little man came bounding through an archway toward him. It was a moment before he could extricate himself, regain his feet and accept the limp, clammy grasp of the hand the man held out to him.

"I'm Bernie Gillespie," the man confided softly. "What's your first name?"

"John," said Johnny. Mr. Gillespie, he noted, wore a Lions Club button.

"Well see here, John," Gillespie said, trying to get an arm around him, "let's just step into my office."

Johnny avoided the embrace. "All I want to know," he said, "is if you sold a casket last night to a lady."

Mr. Gillespie gave him a pained look. "You're not *bereaved?*"

"No," Johnny said.

Gillespie shrugged disappointedly. "Well, yes," he said after a moment, "I did sell a casket to a lady last night Why do you ask?"

"I'm a friend of hers," Johnny said. "Could you tell me what time she came in here?"

The lady had phoned him about nine-thirty, Gillespie said. She had been phoning all the mortuaries, trying to find one open, and he had happened to be in his office doing some paper work. The lady had told him that a relative of hers had died at a little town out in the desert and she wanted to take a casket out there that night. About half an hour later she and a man in a beret had come in. They had asked for the lightest casket he had in stock and he had sold them a molded-aluminum model, retailing at four hundred. A couple of kids could carry that one, Gillespie declared—if, of course, the deceased wasn't too heavy.

❧   ❧   ❧

Johnny went next to the address printed on the pawn ticket, a place off Fremont in the central section, obviously located there to cater to those who went broke in the surrounding gambling establishments. For that reason it was open late at night.

He showed the pawn ticket and the man got the ring out of the safe. Mrs. Taliaferro had borrowed twenty-five hundred on it, according to the paper she had signed. And, looking at that emerald and the size and quality of the diamonds around it, Johnny figured it was worth at least four times that much.

"When did the lady come in with it?" he asked.

"Around nine-thirty last night," the man said. "It ain't hot, is it?"

"No, just a little warm maybe." Johnny took back the pawn ticket. "The guy it belongs to will pay the loan and pick it up," he said. "Maybe tonight."

It all checked out, he thought. Everything did, even what the maid Letty had said. She had told him that just before Sig and Mrs. Taliaferro drove her into town she thought Mrs. Taliaferro had received another phone call, which, according to Mrs. Taliaferro, would have been from Mira.

But the lady had lied to him before, more than once. And he never believed them, once they had lied. So, after he left the pawn shop, he had a bowl of chili and a bottle of beer, and while he sat there he thought it all over, everything that had happened since he came there, all that had been said. And he knew, with three clients depending on him, he had to be absolutely sure. The honor and integrity of Gerard Secret Service, he felt, were at stake. And there was also the fact, of course, that the case had two heads—or more. There was the case of the lady who had vanished and there was the blackmail case. And there was, under the sub-heading of unexplained events, the car that had followed them that afternoon, which did not seem to him to fit in anywhere. And finally, there was the beating he had taken in his motel room. Who and where did that fit?

Now as he sat there and finished his beer he had the feeling that so far he had accomplished little, solved almost nothing. Really, he thought, he hadn't even started yet.

When he went out the last gray light was fading and the neon had begun to fight the night. The cars were stacked, the bars were full and a sporting, transient gentry thronged the street. He went into a drugstore phone booth and called Mitch Barry. Barry had received no further message from the blackmailer.

"Where've you been?" he asked Johnny.

"Looking for that lady friend of yours," Johnny told him.

"You got news for me, Church?"

"Maybe," Johnny said. "I'll check with you later in the evening."

"What do I say if that photographer calls again?"

"Tell him to call you tomorrow," Johnny said. He broke the connection then and dialed his motel.

Both Whitney and Hamilton Sprague had checked in that afternoon, the operator said, and both had been trying to reach him.

"Which one do you want me to connect you with first?" the lady asked him.

"Neither," he said. "Please tell them I'm on the job and I'll get in touch later."

Leaving the drugstore, he walked along Fremont until he came to a hardware store. He went in there and bought a short-handled spade.

He had parked his car on the side street where the pawn shop was and he was starting to unlock the trunk to put the spade in when he saw Beecroft, the lawyer. That red-headed rattlesnake was sitting all alone in a car parked across the street and though he seemed to look right at Johnny he gave no sign that he recognized him.

The trunk, it turned out, had not been locked, or the lock was broken. Anyhow, when he lifted it, he saw there was no room in there for the spade because the luggage area was completely taken up by a body. The body was curled in a fetal position and he couldn't see the face because of the hat that was jammed down over it. But he could see the bloody shirt front.

He let the door drop shut and stood staring at it numbly for a moment. And in that moment he noted the place where scarred paint and curled metal showed the lock had been jimmied. Then he tossed the spade into the back seat, started the car and drove away from there.

CHAPTER FOURTEEN

T HOUGH THERE WERE LIGHTS behind him he could swear his elaborate evasive tactics must have shaken off any tailing car. He had circled blocks, gone south and east before he started north on the Tonopah road again, and now that he had a little time to think about the body in the rear it didn't take him long to make a guess as to whose it was and who had put it there. And if he was right, he thought, some things just might start falling into place.

And yet he had to wait to find out. He made the long drive out to the dude ranch and then along the dirt road to the trail that led into the little canyon before he opened the trunk to make his gruesome check. He flashed his light in, pulled the hat up off the face and a pair of black eyes, glazed with death, stared back at him. His guess had been right. It was, or had been, the man he had met the night before at the front door of the pink house.

"So—" he said. "You went calling again, Mr. Nick." He pushed aside the shirt to look at the wound, and he saw that it had been made by a knife. He shut the trunk then and started up the trail into the canyon with his spade.

In the canyon the wind was moaning in the crevices and there was a sound of wings beating upward as he and his light came flashing in. He located the artfully arranged stones and wildflowers and after he had moved the stones he set the flashlight down on a rock so that its beam fell upon the area of the grave. He began to dig.

It wasn't easy digging in the sand because it was very dry and loose and kept sliding into the excavation he was making. After a while he began to perspire and he took off his jacket and laid it beside the light. Then, soon after he resumed his digging, he thought he heard a sound toward the mouth of the canyon, a footstep, a stone hitting against another, and he dropped the spade and started to spring for the flashlight to snap it off. But a voice stopped him.

"Hold it!" the voice yelled. "You're covered!"

He discarded the idea of doing any moving then. He was in the light, they weren't.

"Lift your hands above your head!" the voice snapped, and the steps were closer now. "We're sheriff's deputies, mister!"

"Toss a badge into the light for me to see," he suggested.

"Lift them."

So he did—what else? Slowly, reluctantly, he lifted them. Then one man stepped within the circle of the light, while the other moved off at an angle, circling the light to come up behind him. The man who faced him wore a gray suit and a sport shirt. He was of medium height with heavy shoulders and his face was big and tough. His hands were big, so big the .38 he held looked lost.

"You're not deputies," Johnny said.

"So?" the man asked. "Want to make something of it?"

"Make a move now and you get it in the back," the one behind him said. A hand reached forward and snatched the Magnum from its holster. Then he was clubbed on the side of the head with the gun, knocked to his knees in the hole he had dug.

When he got up the man who had hit him was taking off his coat. He laid the coat down by the light and tossed the Magnum and his own gun down on it. He was built much like the other man, not tall but big, heavy-shouldered, thick of girth. He had blond, crew-cut hair and protruding teeth that gave him the appearance of grinning when he wasn't.

"Let's you tell us some things," he said. "First, who were the women you come out here with today?"

"And what the hell you diggin' that *hole* for?" the other man demanded. He stuck his gun in the waistband of his pants, and when Johnny just stood there and didn't answer he said, "Okay, Ed. Work on him! Loosen up his tongue."

The one called Ed came at him then. The man feinted with his left and swung a right that never landed because John Church, in all his fury, beat him to the punch, sent him reeling back with a left that skinned his knuckles on those protruding teeth. Then he leaped from his hole and delivered a terrible, perfectly timed right to the jaw, caught the man off balance and sent him crashing down among the rocks.

The other one was ready when Johnny turned and rushed him. He was surprised but ready, and there was a confident contempt in the fact that he did not draw his gun. And he was good. He greeted Johnny with a snaky left that jarred him, then he got him in close, clubbing him with those big fists, hurling him back and down.

Johnny shook his head to clear it. Keep him away, he thought. That's the way to beat him. Don't let him get in close again. He would have gotten up at that moment, but a new voice from the darkness stopped him.

"Now you men quit it!" the voice cried. "Mr. Church, ah'm holding a gun that's looking right at you. You just stay where you are."

There was a sound of steps and in a moment Beecroft appeared in the light. He looked over at the prone figure. "Charlie," he said, "what's wrong with Ed?"

Charlie shrugged and went over and knelt by the other man. "Hit his head," he said after a moment. "He's coming around."

Beecroft glanced at the hole and the spade. "Mister," he told Johnny, "you got some talking to do."

"Why?" Johnny asked. "What is all this?"

Beecroft sat down on a rock. "I just looked in the trunk of that car you're driving," he said softly. He nodded at the hole. "Digging a grave for him, are you?"

"No," Johnny said.

"Then why in hell are you way out here in the desert at night digging a hole!" Beecroft exclaimed in an outraged voice. "You expect to find uranium or something? What were you doing out here today with those women?"

Johnny looked at his watch. "Listen—" he said. "What's your angle? What are you after?"

"Ah want to find *her,*" Beecroft said intently. "Ah've *got* to find her."

"Well," Johnny told him, "that's also my objective. So why are your boys knocking me around?"

"That first time was an accident," Beecroft declared hastily. "At your motel. Ah realized next day that there could be no harm in having you look for her too. But now you're certainly on to something, or into something! What's happening? Ah mean to know!"

"I'm looking for *her,*" Johnny said.

"*Here!*" Beecroft demanded incredulously. "Are you insane?"

"Maybe."

"Did you kill Nick Gardelli?"

"No," Johnny told him. "This is the first time I even heard his whole name. Who is he?"

"A gambler," Beecroft said. "He owns a piece of a place on The Strip. Who did kill him?"

"That we'll come to," Johnny said. "Right now time is short. If you want to find her you're going to have to play along with me. And, if I seem crazy, humor me."

Beecroft gazed at him. "All right," he said after a moment. "Ah saw you with that spade when you looked in the trunk. Unless you were putting it on real good, you were sure enough surprised by what you saw. That's why ah looked in there just a bit ago myself." He nodded. "Okay. Tell me what's going on."

"First," Johnny said, getting up, "I've got to dig some more."

He went over to the hole, picked up his spade and began to dig again. The one called Ed was sitting up now holding his head in his hands. It was clear he was in no condition to take an interest in the proceedings, but Beecroft and Charlie looked on with a puzzled fascination as the sand came flying from the hole. And when, after a few minutes of digging, the spade scraped on metal they jumped up and came over to look.

While Johnny went on digging Beecroft got out a flashlight and held it shining down into the hole. "My God, it's a casket!" he exclaimed. He leaned down and seized Johnny by an arm. "Who is it?" He gazed into Johnny's eyes for a moment and then a terrible look came over his face. *"Oh, no!"* he whispered, "not *her!"*

"That's what they tell me," Johnny said. He knelt, felt along under the edge of the casket lid and found a wing nut.

"Who tells you!" Beecroft screamed.

Johnny glanced up at him. "Her mother and her sisters," he said, unscrewing the nut.

"Her mother and sisters—" Beecroft repeated in a dazed voice. "You mean," he went on, "Somebody just brought her out here and *buried* her."

"She died first, they say."

"No!" Beecroft wailed. And now a sob escaped him and he screamed again. "What are you doing!"

"I'm going to take the lid off this coffin," Johnny said.

Beecroft started to leap down into the hole. "Don't you dare!"

Johnny ignored him. He found another wing nut and began unscrewing it.

"Man—" Beecroft sobbed, "you can't do it."

"You don't have to watch," Johnny told him "Me, I've been paid to find her and I'm going to find her."

"Come on, boss," the one called Charlie said to Beecroft He took hold of Beecroft's arm. "Let's you and me take a stroll."

Beecroft, his shoulders shaking, allowed himself to be led away. Johnny located another nut and now an eerie trepidation seized him. Perhaps everything wasn't the way he had figured it, he thought. Perhaps his conclusions—triggered by that body— about the Taliaferros and their retainer were untrue. If so, he had violated their confidence and his promise of secrecy, even as he now proposed to violate this pitiful grave to which they had led him.

When he had unscrewed the last nut he climbed out of the hole and stood there beside it. He wasn't perspiring now. He felt cold, and that little wind was moaning again high in the rock and the pale owl eyes were watching.

If she *were* in there, if he should lift that casket lid and find her he might as well turn in his license, he thought. For he knew he would never recover from the shock. And now his reluctance to open the casket was growing so great that he realized he must do it quickly or not at all.

He knelt, reached down and pulled the lid up so that it was tilted against the other side of the hole. As he did this he could not resist the impulse to shut his eyes, and when the lid fell back he had a quick, dismaying sense of calamity, for now that haunting scent of hers was unmistakably there.

When he opened his eyes he did so fully expecting to look upon her dead face. Yet, as it turned out, there was nothing in the casket except a white scarf.

He picked up the scarf and for a moment he stood holding it. And he recognized that the relief he felt was due not only to the fact that he had made the right guess about the casket being empty, but was also because she wasn't dead, because somewhere she still existed for him to find, at last to look upon.

CHAPTER FIFTEEN

THERE WAS NO HOPE of shaking Beecroft. When Beecroft learned that the casket was empty he rushed over to the hole and stood staring down, exclaiming, "Oh, thank God! Thank God!" Then he grabbed Johnny, who, without interference from anybody, had picked up his gun and put on his coat, and he demanded an explanation of everything.

There was a real rush on now, Johnny advised him. There was no time to waste. But if the rattlesnake wanted to ride back to town with him, he said, he'd give him the particulars on the way.

Ed, the one who had hit his head on the rock, had had it. Charlie, the other, had to help him out of the canyon and along the road to Beecroft's car. As Johnny had thought, nobody had tailed him out there. He had ditched them in the town, Beecroft said. But after seeing that spade, Beecroft had followed a hunch and they had come out there to the dude ranch, where Ed and Charlie had followed the station wagon that afternoon. They had come along the dirt road with only their parking lights on and found his car.

He didn't spare the horsepower on the way into town and because Beecroft had him over a barrel, knowing of that body in the trunk, he felt obliged to tell him just about everything, as well as most of his speculations and conclusions concerning same, including how the body had got where it was. He didn't mention Mitch Barry, by name, however, in speaking of the blackmail try.

As for Beecroft, he said he hadn't been sleeping nights due to anxiety over the whereabouts of the lady and when the manager of the Panamint Drive apartment house had informed him that morning that either she or some other party had come and taken the things from her apartment he had, Beecroft declared, gone absolutely loco. Did Johnny really think she was still there in town.

Johnny said that if the rest of them were still there he was pretty sure she was. Actually, though, the way he had it worked out, he didn't expect to find any of them still hanging around. And when he tore up the knoll and stopped in front of the pink house he saw that he was only minutes away from being right. The station wagon was near the front door, the door was open and the twins were just carrying out a couple of suitcases.

He parked in front of the station wagon and asked Beecroft to wait until he called for him and, as he got out, that strong-arm Charlie came up the drive in Beecroft's car and went on past, parking behind the station wagon in front of the garage.

"Why, it's Mr. Church again," Lu said, as he approached.

"Did you forget something?" Anne asked him.

"No," he said, "you did." He took the white scarf from his pocket and held it out to them, saw their faces freeze. Then they broke for the house, but he was on their heels and went through the door with them.

Mrs. Taliaferro was entering the living room with another suitcase when he and the twins came in.

"Mr. Church." the lady exclaimed angrily. "May I ask what you are doing here?"

He didn't answer that. He just tossed the scarf down on the table in front of the couch and, when her gaze returned to him after exchanging a stunned glance with her daughters, he said, "*Where* is she?"

"Oh, you cad!" she exclaimed softly. She looked at the scarf again. "This is incredible. You couldn't have."

"You're nothing but a grave robber!" Lu said.

"You're a ghoul!" Anne told him.

"Where is she?" he repeated.

"How could you *believe* she wasn't there," Anne went on. "After all the trouble we went to, buying that casket and—"

"Never mind," Mrs. Taliaferro broke in. She gazed at Johnny. "She's gone," she said.

"Gone where?"

"I don't know."

"Don't give me that!" he said. He drew the Magnum and at the same moment he saw the spot on the white rug. Someone had scrubbed at the spot, but it still retained a rosy tinge and, for his money, had been blood.

"Where's your man, Sig?" he asked.

"Gone," Mrs. Taliaferro said.

"That's another thing I don't believe," he told her. "Lady, whether you like it or not, I'm going to search this house."

She shrugged. "Why waste your time?" She crossed then to the desk and picked up a piece of paper. "He was gone when we got back this afternoon," she said. "He left this note." She handed it to him. "And I wish you'd put that gun away," she added. "We're sufficiently impressed now, I think. Aren't we, girls?"

They nodded. "Quite," Anne said.

Johnny read the note. *"No more need for you to worry, my lady,"* it said. And that was all. It was signed *Sig.*

He dropped the note on the table with the scarf, and for a moment he stared thoughtfully at the two items. Then he tucked his gun back in its holster and sat down. "I'm going to tell you some things now," he said, "none of which will be news to you, I'm sure."

He gazed at Mrs. Taliaferro. "To begin with," he told her, "I figure you've been operating a kind of romantic con game with your daughter Mira for a long time. You had your Taliaferro, who soured you on men for good. She had her Cheever. So you've both been getting even with the men through these capers and, incidently, supporting yourselves in great style. But gambling is your kick, like you told me, and I figure you got behind. You maybe signed some tabs—some I.O.U's. You always had money. You've been here before, so your credit was good. At least with Nick Gardelli it was."

He was watching her carefully now and he saw her wince at the name, saw a wave of shock run through her. "Am I right?" he demanded.

"Who told you this?" she asked.

"Never mind," he said. "Anyhow, you weren't too worried because you thought your Mira was going to get that hundred grand from Whitney."

"Who *told* you?"

"Whitney!" he snapped.

"You talked to Nick Gardelli too?"

He thought a minute. "Yes," he said, "I talked to him. Anyhow, when you learned Whitney had the marriage annulled and the bequest canceled, you were desperate, because you were in but deep with Gardelli—about twenty G's, say—and he was getting nasty. I figure you had gambled away the money you got for that Jag my client supplied and were down to the ring. It wouldn't bring enough to pay Gardelli and no new sucker was likely to toss your Mira that kind of money on a few days' acquaintance, no matter how good she was. So—" He paused, staring at her. "You tried blackmail. Right?"

"No!" she said. "I swear by all that's holy, I don't know what you are talking about when you mention that word."

"Your man Sig took a compromising photograph of Mira with Mitch Barry," he said. "Naturally he, or you, ma'am, wouldn't want a picture like that of her floating around. That's why you cut the heads out."

Mrs. Taliaferro and her daughters exchanged a wild look. "I *don't* know what you're talking about," Mrs. Taliaferro repeated. "I haven't been involved with any blackmail and I'm sure Sig would never do anything like that."

"Since I know he killed Nick Gardelli, how can you expect me to believe he'd stop at blackmail?" Johnny asked her.

"*Killed* him!" she whispered. Then both she and the twins stared at the spot on the rug.

Johnny waited, watching them. "Your Sig arranged a rendezvous last night to collect twenty grand from Barry," he went on after a moment. "But he got shot at and ran. That was the end of the blackmail try."

Mrs. Taliaferro started to say something in protest at that point, but he lifted a hand, stopping her. "I'm sorry," he told her, "but I'm afraid it doesn't make much difference now what you say. Things figure. When Sig got no blackmail money out of Barry there was only one chance left. Your Mira had to try another caper quick. Maybe you had a new victim already lined up. But to operate you *had* to get me out of town. Therefore, the casket, the phony burial. And I will admit it took imagination to figure that one out. Still it was right in line with everything else you've handed me, lady. You've *never* given me anything yet but deception. What I mean to say is, you really lie with a great deal of imagination, ma'am."

"I'm not lying about the blackmail," she said. "And what I was trying to tell you was that if you knew Sig you'd know he wasn't capable of anything like that."

A faint doubt struck him. "Why?" he said. "Tell me about him. Where did you pick him up?"

"At Cannes," she said. "After the war. He's a Bulgarian. He had drifted down there and was doing odd jobs. He went to work for me."

"Mother had to hire him," Lu said. "He would follow her around like a dog, just sit and stare at her, wait places for hours just to get a glimpse of her. Sig worships her."

Anne sobbed. "Poor Sig."

"What I'm trying to tell you," Mrs. Taliaferro went on, "is that Sig just wouldn't be *capable* of blackmail. He neither speaks nor writes English too well—as you may see by that note—and he simply wouldn't have the mentality for it."

The doubt grew stronger, yet he felt he couldn't afford it. This just *had* to be. "You could do his writing for him," he said. "Even his talking. The voice on the phone was disguised. And as I know so well by now, you're all really great at acting."

"No," she said, shaking her head. "No, Mr. Church. You're wrong!"

"Well," he said, "we'll skip the blackmail for the moment. Anyhow, you waved good-by to me this afternoon, thinking you were waving me onto the next plane back to San Francisco." He gave her a hard, steady look. "Now don't tell me that's a lie!"

She shrugged. "Think what you want, dear sir."

"Then you came into the house," he went on. "You found the note and saw that spot on the rug. You had a hunch just *why* Sig wrote that there was no more need for you to worry, why he had bugged out. And, after you thought it over a while, you decided you'd better bug out too."

"We should have bugged faster, it seems," Lu remarked, gazing at him.

"You really hang on, don't you, Mr. Church?" Anne said. "Tell me—*why* do you want to keep making so much trouble for us?"

"It's his career!" Mrs. Taliaferro exclaimed. "Persecuting helpless women!"

"Suppose Sig *did* kill this man that Mother owed the money to," Lu said. "That's something *Sig* did. You can't very well blame us for the poor creature's acts."

"Who said I was?" Johnny asked her.

Anne said, "Well, then, what's your *angle,* mister? What do you want from us?"

"Her," he said.

"What do you plan to do to her?" Lu asked.

"I want to see her and talk to her. That's all I've wanted to do from the beginning."

"Well," Anne said, "why don't you *let* him, Mother? I can't understand why you didn't in the first place."

"Because I didn't know where to find her!" Mrs. Taliaferro snapped angrily. "And she was ill, *still* is. Remember that, will you please? And besides, she was too frightened by that picture-taking business. We didn't know what was going on, what this man here was really up to."

Johnny said quietly, "Ma'am, I'm telling you—you produce her now, or ten minutes from now you are going to be talking to some policemen about a man who was murdered here. And even if you do get in the clear, you won't be going anywhere for a while."

Mrs. Taliaferro gazed at him. "Suppose I let you see her," she said. "Then what? Will you allow us to leave without further interference?"

He shook his head. "I don't have to bargain with you," he told her. "You produce her, ma'am, or else."

"Let him see her," Anne urged her mother.

"She's ill!" Mrs. Taliaferro said. "This climate doesn't agree with her. We've got to get her away from here."

"He could see her just a few minutes," Anne said. "Then I'm sure he'll let us finish packing and leave. We'll take her to the mountains."

"Mr. Beecroft, her lawyer, wants to see her too," Johnny said. "He's waiting outside in my car."

"Oh, no!" Mrs. Taliaferro exclaimed. "That's too much!"

"He'll make trouble if he doesn't see her."

"Oh, Mother—what's the difference?" Anne said.

"Mr. Sprague, my San Francisco client, is here in town and he would also like to see her," Johnny said.

"Oh, no!" Mrs. Taliaferro wailed.

"He'll make trouble too if he doesn't get to see her."

"Go *on*, Mother," Anne said. "What's the diff?"

"And Mr. Whitney is here," Johnny went on. "He flew in from Chicago today just for a few words with her. Who knows? Maybe he'll give her some of that money, after all. And as long as she's receiving, Mitch Barry would also like to see her."

"Oh, *great!*" Lu exclaimed. Then she asked Johnny quickly, "He wasn't in that other car that came, was he?"

"No," Johnny said. He looked at Mrs. Taliaferro. "With your permission, ma'am, I'd like to phone those gentlemen now."

For a long moment Mrs. Taliaferro was silent and as she stared at him those gray-green eyes of hers glittered with a dislike so intense that he felt almost singed by it. "All right," she said finally. "Go ahead—telephone. You shall see her—all of you! But you've got to give her at least ten minutes to get ready for callers. She's in bed. She has been taking a nap while we packed and I'll have to wake her." Her voice broke then and the fire in the eyes that looked at John Church was hotter. "If you possessed one iota of humanity," she cried at him, "you wouldn't do this!"

"Yes, ma'am," he agreed, and he moved past her toward the phone.

CHAPTER SIXTEEN

WHEN THE THREE GENTLEMEN learned that the lost lady had positively been located and that they—by courtesy of Gerard Secret Service Agency, Branches Throughout the World—were to see her in ten minutes time at the pink house on Heavenly Knoll, they sounded fairly dazed with delight. And though he was aware of a similar feeling, John Church was also ridden by the knowledge that perhaps the most important and really criminal part of the case, the blackmail part, remained unsolved. At least his attempt to pin it on the missing Sig, with or without the help of Mrs. Taliaferro, was certainly inconclusive and in need of evidence.

When he finished making the three phone calls he went outside to his car and told Beecroft the news. Then, in the hope that Sig, in his haste to get away, might have left something of an incriminating nature lying around his room, he went past Beecroft's car with the two men in it into the garage. When he snapped on the light he saw that the stair door was ajar.

There was a light switch at the foot of the stairs and he snapped that on, lighting the room above. Then he went up cautiously, his gun in his hand.

The room, however, was empty. Clearly a servant's room, the furnishings were modest, consisting of a bed, a chair, a table with a lamp on it and a grass rug. The bath also was the plain, strictly utilitarian kind servants got. He opened the cabinet. A bathroom made a good darkroom for developing film and he was looking for a colored bulb. But there was nothing in the cabinet but a used razor blade and a piece of soap. Then he looked in the wastebasket beneath the washbowl and saw the towel. He knew it must have been used to scrub at the spot on the living room rug. The towel was still wet and there was diluted blood and bits of fuzz from the nap of the rug on it.

The towel reminded him that he still had a big problem, namely, that body in the trunk. And while the towel was great evidence in favor of his own innocence, he had no plans to use it. That was one part of the case, he decided, that he wanted absolutely nothing to do with.

He was going back through the bedroom when he heard the garage door being closed. When he reached the foot of the stairs strongarm Charlie was standing there in the middle of the garage under the light.

"I never finished with you," Charlie told him. "Now, boy, for what you done to Ed, I'm really going to maul you."

Johnny paused with one foot still on the bottom step and stared at him. Something the man had said had set a little bell ringing in his brain, but for a minute he couldn't answer the bell. Then suddenly he could.

"—really going to *maul* you." It was that word—the voice!

He moved then. He took off his jacket and his gun, laid them on the bottom step. "That was a great knee job you did on me at the motel," he said.

Charlie grinned. "You like that, boy?"

"I'm telling you. You got a great technique."

"Try a new kind," Charlie said, and as he spoke he lunged, bringing up his right foot, as if he were getting off a quick kick.

This time, though, the football wasn't there. John Church grabbed the foot, twisted and lifted it, and the quick kicker crashed to the concrete floor.

When he got up he ran into a long, looping right that sent him down again and glazed his eyes. This time he never had a chance to get in close with those sledgelike fists of his. Johnny kept him away, kept straightening him up, lashing at his head, never letting him get set. Then after a while he tired of it and put Charlie away with a right hook.

When Charlie opened his eyes Johnny was sitting on his chest. "You were going to maul Mitch Barry too," Johnny told him. "I was listening on the phone when you talked to him. If he got cute and yelled cops, you said, you'd really *maul* him. Now, friend, you want some more of what you just had or are you going to talk?"

Charlie gazed at him from puffed and discolored eyes. "Talk," he muttered weakly.

"What are you? What do you do for a living?"

"Was a deputy," Charlie said. "Me and Ed. We got kicked out."

"So Beecroft hired you to watch the lady and when she took up with Barry you saw a way to make yourself some easy money. Okay, Charlie. Where's that negative?"

Charlie shut his eyes. "Don't know," he said.

"You want some more fists in your face?"

Charlie opened his eyes again. "Beecroft has the negative," he whispered.

"Beecroft!" Johnny stared at him a moment, then he got up. "God help you if you're lying to me," he told him.

Charlie groaned and raised himself to a sitting position. He found a handkerchief and started dabbing at his bloody face. "That's straight," he said. "Beecroft got us to take the picture. His angle was the lady. He figured to blackmail her with that photo, but not for dough, if you get what I mean. He really went for her. We offered to split with him, if he'd let us have a print to make the try on Barry. He agreed, only he made us cut her head out, so we cut out Barry's too."

"Do you know how many prints were made?" Johnny asked him.

"Just the one that I know of," Charlie said. "Beecroft developed it at his apartment the night we did the job. After we cut the heads out he burned them up in an ashtray."

Johnny got his jacket and his gun and when he opened the garage door a taxi, which would have Sprague or Whitney in it, was coming up the drive. He turned back to Charlie then. "You get your pal and take this taxi that's out here to wherever you're going," he told him. "Come on, *move.*"

And now, he thought, I believe I just had a really bright idea.

Hamilton Sprague got out of the taxi and as Johnny went to meet him another taxi arrived with Alan K. Whitney. Johnny, as he shook hands with Sprague, saw Charlie helping his pal, Ed, into the first taxi. Then he introduced himself to Whitney, a plump man in his fifties with a soft and helpless air. At that point, Beecroft got out of Johnny's car to see what was going on and while Johnny was introducing the three surprised men to one another Mitch Barry drove up with his pals.

When Barry, a mystified look on his handsome face, came over to the group Johnny introduced him. He then led the procession up to the door of the pink house and punched the button that sounded the chimes.

Mrs. Taliaferro opened the door almost at once, and he had never seen her looking better, which was saying a lot. In the gentle light of the hallway her chill beauty was quite striking and her manner was so calm and regal that he was aware of the dust on his shoes, the blood on his knuckles and his generally rumpled condition.

"Gentlemen—" Mrs. Taliaferro said grandly, and she was clearly not including him. She was addressing the quartet behind him. "*Do* come in, please," she told them.

As the gentlemen passed him, one by one, Johnny introduced them to the lady. When they were all in the living room Mrs. Taliaferro asked them to be seated and she explained briefly that her daughter Mira had fallen ill and that the poor, wayward creature had at last returned to the bosom of her family which was, Johnny thought, quite an apt expression for that stacked, all-female family. They were taking her to the mountains to convalesce, Mrs. Taliaferro went on, and she asked them not to judge her too harshly and please not to overtax her strength by spending too much time with her, nor to say anything that might upset her.

She looked the gentlemen over then and said, "Mr. Beecroft, I think you should see her first, being her lawyer, and Mr. Whitney, you next. After that Mr. Barry. And finally, Mr. Sprague."

Johnny, who had not sat down, watched Beecroft, with a flushed and eager look, jump up from his chair, saw Mrs. Taliaferro escort him down the hall toward that patio bedroom and for a moment he stood wondering why she had selected the gentlemen in just that order. Then he turned, went back through the entry and out the front door to his car. Mitch Barry's boys, he saw, had turned the Cad and were now parked down the drive out of his way.

He drove up past the garage and backed until he was a couple of feet from the rear of Beecroft's car. He got out then, took Beecroft's keys from the ignition and opened the trunk. After that he opened the trunk of his own car. When he was finished with the operation he didn't have a body any more. Beecroft did.

And now, as he waited just inside the dark garage, he reflected that you didn't necessarily have to be the law to see that justice was done.

He waited there about five minutes, then he heard the front door of the house open and shut, heard steps coming along the drive. It was Beecroft and as he approached Johnny could hear him sniffling and mumbling.

"She really liked me *most* deeply," he heard Beecroft say. "But it can't be!" There was a sob then and when Beecroft reached the door of his car he got out a handkerchief and blew his nose. "Oh, that kiss!" he whispered. Then John Church stepped from the garage and hit him. He caught the body as it sagged and dragged it into the garage.

He found the negative in one of the compartments of Beecroft's wallet and for a minute he stared at it, holding it up to his flashlight, seeing the dark faces, the white heads of hair and, even in the negative, he thought, beneath the expression of blank surprise, you could discern her beauty, sense her strangeness.

Beecroft had begun to groan with returning conscious-ness by then, so he slipped the negative in his own breast pocket and got out of there.

When he went back into the house Whitney, who had lipstick on one cheek, was standing at the telephone with tears stream-ing down his face phoning for a taxi. Barry had vanished and he could see Mrs. Taliaferro hovering in the hall near the closed door of that patio bedroom.

He went over to where Hamilton Sprague sat perspiring and gave him the pawn ticket for his ring, telling him the amount of the pledge, but Sprague was so nervous and distracted he didn't think the man even heard him. And it was the same with Whitney when he walked to the door with him as Whitney went out to wait for his taxi. He told the old boy he would see him later at the motel, but Whitney merely gave him a damp, vague glance and went on out.

And now he was beginning to get the nerves too. Only Sprague left now, he thought, then *me!* And, despite the air conditioning, it was hot in there. For a while he paced, looking down the hall toward that bedroom door near which Mrs. Taliaferro now sat in a basket chair, staring at the door and apparently trying to listen.

What was Barry doing in there so long!

He paced on over to the tall white doors that led out to the pool and opened them. The breeze had died, the sky was clear, with the stars mirrored in the pool. After a moment he went out and strolled up along the side of the pool, passing through the parallelograms of light streaming from the twins' bedrooms. The twins had finished their packing, the last of their luggage stood waiting to be carried out, and their rooms now reminded him of hotel bedrooms when you took that last look around to see if you had left anything.

As he moved back toward the doors he heard Mrs. Taliaferro's voice and when he entered Barry was emerging from the hall. Barry's tie was askew, his hair was mussed and he was dabbing absently at the lipstick on his mouth with a handkerchief.

"You shouldn't have kept her so long!" Mrs. Taliaferro said behind him. "I'm sure you tired her." She stopped at the entrance to the living room. "Mr. Sprague!" she called, and Hamilton Sprague popped up trembling from his chair.

Johnny walked over and intercepted Barry as Sprague went off with Mrs. Taliaferro. "You can stop worrying now," he told Barry. He handed him the negative and, though Barry looked at it, apparently recognized it for what it was and understood what he had said, it was clear that nothing could really penetrate those trailing wisps of female glory that still swirled about him. He even smelled of her, Johnny thought.

"Well," he said, with more than a touch of envy, "looks like you might have got a fast sample of what you never got before."

Barry shook his head dreamily. "So close," he whispered. Then he appeared to shrug off some of the drug. "But that's no cigar," he declared in a sad and wistful way.

"Maybe she's just waiting for the right boy to come along," Johnny suggested, but he knew Barry didn't hear him. The Big Name was already on his way toward the front door.

He was perspiring again now. The knowledge that in a few minutes he would be stepping into that bedroom and actually seeing her was doing something to his viscera. He felt his detachment, what critical judgment he possessed, vanishing. And yet there was something that was urgently demanding his thought, something, or perhaps only bits of things, swirling just beyond the border of cognition, striving for his attention. It was like one of those drawings where you followed the dots. He not only couldn't see the drawing, he couldn't even see the dots. He sensed only that they were there, that he *had* seen them.

And now he heard that door open down the hall, heard the steps, saw Sprague, wet-eyed and wiping his glasses, enter. Then Mrs. Taliaferro appeared. She stood staring at him, and in a deep, downbeat way she uttered his name.

And at that point all else vanished from his mind but what he would see when he went into the bedroom down the hall.

"Mr. Church—" Mrs. Taliaferro said again, and when he crossed to her she did not turn, the way she had with the others, and lead him down the hall. Instead, she said to him, "I trust *you* are now satisfied, inasmuch as all your clients are."

He nodded slowly. "It's true that I've got no bone to pick of my own."

"In that case," she said, "I see no purpose in you going in to see Mira. The procession of visitors you summoned has really exhausted her."

"Lady," he told her grimly, "machine guns won't keep me out of there!"

She continued to stare up at him for a moment after he said it, then she exclaimed softly, "Why, you've fallen for her too, haven't you! Oh, you great, heartless brute of a man. Ha! And never even *seen* her. Oh, how right that you never *should!*"

"Lady," he said. "Stand aside!"

Then, as he spoke, the door down the hall was flung open and he saw *her*. She stood against the soft glow of the bedroom light, and it was as if the face of that photograph he had seen on Panamint Drive had come alive. He could see her body outlined against the light through the white negligee she was wearing and the light was shining on her black hair.

"Mother—" she said in the most magnificent voice he had ever heard, soft yet vibrant and laced with hormones. "I want to see him," she said. "Really, I *insist* on it."

CHAPTER SEVENTEEN

WHEN HE WENT into the room the patio doors were opened and there was the fragrance of orange blossoms mingled with her scent. Her luggage from the Panamint Drive apartment was there. She was lying on a chaise, wearing gold sandals and that white silk negligee and there was an orange blossom in her hair.

"Mr. Church—" she said softly, and her eyes held his, as if willing him not to look elsewhere quite yet, for it was clear she wore nothing beneath the negligee, which, with one V plunging perilously downward, another charging daringly upward, promised at any moment the ultimate in disclosures.

He shut the door behind him, leaned against it. As he did so, he snapped the lock. "I don't know what to call you," he told her. "I guess you're not Mrs. Whitney, seeing that the marriage was annulled. Mrs. Cheever?"

"Call me Mira," she said in that thrilling voice. She moved her legs a bit and patted the chaise beside her. "Won't you sit here?"

He nodded, yet he did not move at once. He felt he must, so to speak, catch his breath, recover a little from the shock of her before he got any closer. And now he saw how her face had the same lovely contours as the other Taliaferros'. She had the twins' straight little nose, yet her mouth was different, her entire effect, her expression, her essence—all different. Here, he thought, were darkness and depth, passion mingled with that curious innocence he had noted in the photograph. And here, indeed, was a spirit burning very bright, no longer a shadow that he pursued, a haunting scent, a never-to-be-forgotten face captured by a lens, but flesh and blood and beauty, a lusting, vital virgin of a lady.

She was gazing at him wisely, her lips amused. "Afraid of me?" she asked.

He moved toward the chaise. "Yes," he said. "You see I really found you by following the trail of your victims." Then a thought struck him abruptly, one that should have long before. Was it one of the dots, he wondered, in that undrawn picture?

She patted the chaise again. "Please do sit down. I won't bite you, Church." She laughed. "Excuse me. That's the way the twins refer to you. Oh, I know all about you, Church."

"Your mother said you were sick," he remarked.

"Not *all* the time, Church."

"If you've got TB, like she told me, how come you go around kissing all the men?"

She loosed a peal of laughter and it was one of the most delightful sounds he had ever heard. It was only as it died away that he realized there was sadness in it too. "So that's why you fear me," she said. "You think I'm contagious."

"You're *not?*"

"No," she said. "Believe me, I am not. Listen, Church—I did have TB, not bad, but I had it. However, I was completely cured. This was years ago, in Switzerland, and when I got over it, it was as if I were reborn. But—"

She stopped, gazing at him, and her face now was completely haunted. He had the illusion of a fragility she did not possess, a transience. And suddenly he understood all Hamilton Sprague had tried to tell him.

"To mother," she went on, "it's always as if I still had it, were still the invalid. And I confess, there *is* something strangely wrong with me. Perhaps my metabolism is different than theirs. Perhaps I'm a case for the psychiatry books, one of those multiple personalities. I don't know. All I know is that for a time I *live*, for glorious hours, days, I do! And then I don't live at all. I'm completely dormant. I don't exist. Or perhaps someone else takes me over for a time."

She moved then, reached for the box of gold-tipped cigarettes on the table beside the chaise and, as she did, one firm and lovely breast escaped, only to be enveloped again as she leaned back. He moved then. He went to her and lit her cigarette.

"Can you understand?" she asked him.

"A little." He nodded at the golden sandals. "I know you're not like the rest of your family, anyhow. They go around in their bare feet."

She reached a hand up and drew him down beside her. "Oh, Church," she told him. "You're just as they said, completely unromantic."

He gazed at his hands, the bloody knuckles. The palms were grimed with that red-colored dust from the canyon. "Maybe I'd be more romantic if I was cleaned up a little," he said.

"Poor man!" she exclaimed. "What a chase they've led you. Don't you think that grave was the most superbly macabre idea? And yet it didn't fool you. I can tell you, Church, I admire you. So do the twins."

"I didn't notice," he remarked.

"Poor kids," she said. "They aren't really the sticks they must seem to you. Believe me, they have their moments, but of course you don't see them then. It's Mother who holds them down. Oh, my God, she's so strict with them. They're so frustrated. They're like prisoners, Church."

"I remember having that impression," he said, and he wished she wouldn't talk any more about those twins. The breast appeared again briefly as she leaned over to knock the ashes from her cigarette and he swallowed. Now his eyes surveyed the rest of her, stretched out there so close to him.

"Anne told me she has a case on you," she continued. "Lu's mad about that Barry. Anne said Lu would always make Sig stop the car every time they drove past that picture of Barry at the entrance to the Nevada Grande so that she could sit and gaze at it."

"Seems to me you liked Barry pretty much yourself," he couldn't help saying.

"You're wrong," she told him. She put a hand on his arm then, gazing up at him from beneath her black lashes, and in that light it was impossible to tell exactly what color her eyes were. "Are you glad you found me, Church?"

"Yes," he said. "It was my job."

"Is that the only reason?"

He met her eyes. "No," he said.

"Why?"

"I was curious."

"No more than that?"

"Yes," he said slowly. "More than that. I saw that photograph of you in your apartment."

"*And?*" she whispered.

"Then I *had* to find you."

"Why!" She had flung her cigarette into the ashtray and now one of her hands moved up his arm. "*Why* did you have to find me? You know I'm poison, don't you?"

"I *do.*"

"Yet you might *love* me!"

He didn't answer. He bent over her then and took her in his arms, pressed his lips to that paradoxical, wanton-inno-cent mouth, and in the next instant he really understood what the boys were talking about. You'd never had it till she kissed you. It was better than an entire honeymoon routine with anyone else.

Vaguely after a time he became aware of a rapping on the door and he disengaged, saw that reddish canyon grime from his hands on the silk, on her skin.

"It's only Mother," she whispered. Then she called out to her. "Please go away!" she said. "We're having the most interesting conversation."

"Are you all right?" Mrs. Taliaferro's voice demanded.

"Of course I'm all right!"

John Church rose abruptly and in a drugged and giddy way started for the bathroom.

"Where are you going?" the lady whispered fiercely. "Come back!"

"I've *got* to wash my hands," he said. He opened the door and started through the dressing room, then he saw that the bathroom door was ajar and there was a light on in there. Through the slot he could see Lu, nude, sitting on a vanity bench rubbing cream on her face as she gazed into a mirror. A figure came off the chaise then and grabbed his arm and he pulled the door shut and turned to face her. And now, he saw, the two V's had met.

"Lu wanted to get a peek at Barry!" she whispered.

"Oh," he said, and dots had begun to dance before his eyes, lines were being drawn between the dots, but he really couldn't believe in the picture he saw taking shape.

"Don't mind her! Just *hold* me," she begged him, and once more she came into his arms, flattened her splendid length against him, found his lips again.

For a time they stood there, as if locked in some contest, lost, the lady moaning. Then, finally, his hands began to move along her silken back and one hand slowly, almost reluctantly, kept moving higher, went upward past her shoulders, paused to caress the soft nape of her neck beneath the lustrous black hair, then moved on up into the hair.

And when, gently but firmly, he pulled, the hair came off in his hand—all of it.

CHAPTER EIGHTEEN

FOR A MOMENT, so rapt was she, so deeply sunk in passion's sweet embrace, his companion did not notice the loss of her hair. But, though delayed, the shock, when it did come, struck her no less forcefully and she sprang back, stood staring up at him and that black wig he held aloft with great, gray-green eyes. Then, as if just to make absolutely sure of her loss, she ran her hands through her own chestnut curls and finally she said to him in Anne's voice, "Okay. So you guessed."

He felt like slapping her at first, but after she spoke he didn't, for there was something about her that made him feel sorrier for her than he was feeling at the moment for himself. The dots had fallen into place, the picture was complete and now, fumbling in a pocket for his cigarettes, he went over and sank down on the chaise. Then Anne came over and fell on her knees before him and she had tears in her eyes.

"I'm truly sorry, Church," she said. "But, in a way, I wanted you to know, because, you see, I fell in love with you."

He looked up. "When was this?" he asked, and for a moment he was surprised out of the big shock by this lesser one.

"This afternoon," she told him, "riding out there to the canyon. I fell in love with the back of your head. And I didn't want you to take a look at that grave and go away forever. I tried to give you a couple of hints as to the state of things."

"Like *mirages?*" he suggested.

"Yes," she said. "And I gave you the Mira look once and spoke in her voice. But I played it straight with you tonight. I couldn't let Mira down by not doing my best. And anyway, when I'm Mira, I *am* Mira."

"That's when you *live?*"

"Yes," she said, "even though Mother always makes us pick old ones."

"How about Barry?"

"That was a mistake," she said. "I had Sprague, then Mother was desperate for cash. It was Lu's turn to be Mira and she had to get a new one quick—"

"Ah," he said, "I get it. Lu was Mira for Beecroft, for Whitney and Barry. She was the one getting the divorce, who had to take that apartment to establish residence."

"Yes," she said. "We play Mira slightly differently. Anyhow, Lu was sitting there at the Nevada Grande waiting for an old one when Barry moved in. Not that Lu was sorry, of course. And at least he seemed to qualify from the money angle."

He nodded, remembering Lu's eagerness to know if Barry was in that other car that had driven up. And now he was ready for the pay-off question. "Where *is* Mira?" he asked.

Anne gazed at him and, even without the wig, he had the illusion again of that haunted one. "Dead," she said softly. "She died at a sanatarium in Switzerland of TB and heartbreak eight years ago. Right after Cheever left her."

He said roughly then, "How did you happen to get started on this big playing-Mira kick? You think it's fair to her?"

"Oh, *yes!*" she said. "Don't you see, it's a kind of immortality! And we don't do anything to shame her. We never let a man—well—*never*. Even if we should want to. We just couldn't, you see—not as *Mira*. We loved our Mira. We worshiped her so much that we were always imitating her, and we looked like her, except that she had our father's black hair and dark eyes. After she died I was playing her one day, just because I missed her so much and wanted her back so much and that was what gave Mother the idea."

She paused, rubbed a finger over his skinned knuckles. "How did you guess?"

He said thoughtfully after a moment, "All along the key to this case—I mean as far as you Taliaferros are concerned—has been one thing: *Deception*. Nothing has ever turned out to be what it seemed to be. It's been just one false front, one new hoax, one lying story after another, ending up with that empty casket."

"Remember," she said, "that first time you came Mira was supposed to be only a friend. Mother figured that when you couldn't find her you'd go on back to San Francisco and not bother us again. She was desperate then for money because we had learned about what Whitney had done. And we were scared, too, because of that picture-taking. But Mother had to pay off Gardelli. If she skipped town without paying him she'd never be able to gamble again because she'd have the reputation as a welcher. Besides that, Gardelli might have had her bumped off."

"Your mother had Sig follow me that first day," he suggested.

She nodded. "Sig saw you go to Beecroft's office. Later he followed you to her apartment and he came back that night and said some men had taken you to Barry's. So when you came here the next day and talked about blackmail and the D.A., we just didn't know what was going on. We couldn't get *her* involved in anything like that. What we had to do was to satisfy you in some way, get you out of town, because Mother's only chance to get enough money to pay off Gardelli by that time was for Mira to have another affair with someone really rich."

He nodded. "So the casket," he said. "Then when you came back this evening and got Sig's note, you saw that spot. You added the two together and started packing."

"Then you—you heartless, unsentimental bloodhound—*you* appeared," she said. "And though I gave no sign, my heart leaped." She gazed up at him. "Church—" she whispered, running a fingertip over his knuckles, "did you *like* kissing me?"

He nodded. "I did."

"You did, I know, because you thought you were kissing *her*," she said. "But, don't you see, really and truly it was *me* you were kissing. It was *my* lips, *my* passion, *my* body in your arms. Oh, Church! It's always Mira. She's the one they love. Couldn't someone love just *me*?"

"Don't you ever have any boy friends of your own?" he asked after a moment.

"No," she said. "Mother wouldn't allow it, for one thing. And it would be difficult to form any kind of an attachment when we're always busy playing Mira."

He gazed at her. "Good God!" he said gently then. He rose, brought her up with him, held her.

"Please," she whispered, straining against him. *"Love* me, Church!"

"Yes," he said. And when he kissed her now he knew at once that it wasn't the wig that had made her so good. And of course now she did not have the wig to restrain her.

There was another pounding on the door. Mrs. Taliaferro's voice called, and the one lying in his arms became Mira briefly again, answering her mother sharply in Mira's voice, telling her to please go away.

Then after a moment, Anne's voice whispered, "Church, dearest, take me back to San Francisco with you!"

He didn't say anything right away to that. He lay and thought it over, having definite knowledge now of just how much there was in favor of it.

"*Please* do."

"No," he told her finally. "It wouldn't be any good."

"Why?"

"If you had really buried her out there," he said, "I think I would take you."

"What do you mean?"

"I mean she's your life," he said. "You know that. You couldn't live without her. And with you around, I'd never forget her."

"You want to forget her?"

He reached for the switch, turned on the lamp and got up. "I want to keep her the way she was."

"Unattainable?"

"Something like that," he agreed. Then abruptly he crossed to the door. "Good-by, Anne."

"Good-by, Church," she whispered after a moment, and there were tears in her eyes.

He turned, facing the door. "I guess she'd better tell me good-by too," he said.

Behind him he heard her moving and presently that other, that never-to-be-forgotten voice called softly, vibrantly, "Church!" And when he turned he saw *her* standing there against the light again, saw that haunting face, and now her eyes were blazing with triumph as she looked at him.

"You'll *never* forget me," she said deeply. "Never forget me, never possess me! Never, Church, till the day you die!"

For a long moment he stood staring into her face and when at last he turned away and went out of there he knew that it was true. He went blindly by Mrs. Taliaferro, who started to say something, then looked into his face and fell silent. And it was as if that Mira followed him out, a lovely essence, a heartbreak, passing with him into the desert night.

THE END

www.ingramcontent.com/pod-product-compliance
Lightning Source LLC
Chambersburg PA
CBHW030350180626
46812CB00007B/2833